Shakespeare's Tales

Shakespeare's Tales

RETOLD BY
BEVERLEY BIRCH

ILLUSTRATED BY
STEPHEN LAMBERT

h
Hodder
Children's
Books

A division of Hachette Children's Books

For Thomas and Ben – B.B

First published in 2002
by Hodder Children's Books

This edition published in 2008

Text copyright © Beverley Birch 2002
Illustrations copyright © Stephen Lambert 2002

Hodder Children's Books
338 Euston Road
London NW1 3BH

Hodder Children's Books Australia
Level 17/207 Kent Street
Sydney NSW 2000

A catalogue record of this book is available from the British Library.

ISBN: 978 0 340 97012 6
10 9 8 7 6 5 4 3 2 1

Printed in China

Hodder Children's Books is a division of Hachette Children's Books
An Hachette Livre UK Company
www.hachettelivre.co.uk

CONTENTS

Hamlet 7

Antony and Cleopatra 41

Othello 71

The Tempest 99

HAMLET

Hᴵɢʜ ᴏɴ ᴛʜᴇ ᴛᴏᴡᴇʀs ᴏғ Eʟsɪɴᴏʀᴇ, royal castle to the kings of Denmark, three men stood in the bitter winds of a chill night. Far below, an angry sea crashed and pounded at the rocks. But it was not that booming menace, nor the midnight gloom that kept them close together, searching the darkness with wary eyes.

'What, has this thing appeared again tonight?' Marcellus asked Bernardo, his fellow Officer of the Watch.

'I have seen nothing,' Bernardo answered, and looked beyond Marcellus uneasily. Their friend, Horatio, leaned on the parapet and watched the turbulent seas below.

'Horatio says it is our fantasy, and will not let belief take hold of him,' Marcellus told Bernardo, stamping his feet and blowing on his icy hands. 'If the apparition comes ...'

'Tush, tush, it will not appear,' Horatio shook his head. He tugged his cloak about him, hunching his shoulders against the wind. Their tale could certainly not be believed: a ghostly figure stalking the battlements by night! This strange story was the only greeting from his anxious friends on his arrival here in Elsinore from Wittenberg. Yet he saw how this bleak platform, suspended above a raging sea, could plant such tremors even in a soldier's mind.

'Look!' Marcellus' cry sliced through the darkness. 'Look where it comes again!'

'Just like the king that's dead!' Bernardo whispered across the quivering silence.

Horatio looked, but saw only a mist that curled across the battlements towards them.

Then he looked again. All certainty was numbed, all understanding fled, for through the icy curtain a looming figure moved. It trod the swirling mists with soundless march: no clink of metal or scrape of boot on stone, only the great figure's silent, majestic tread. As it neared, it turned its face towards them and what a sorrow swelled within that bloodless face!

Bernardo seized Horatio's arm. 'Does it not look just like the king?'

For a long moment Horatio could not speak.

'Most like,' he whispered. 'It fills me with fear and wonder.'

'It wants to be spoken to,' Bernardo said.

'Question it, Horatio,' urged Marcellus.

Horatio shook off the numbing fear and raised his voice with loud determination. 'What are you? By heaven, speak!' His voice echoed across the battlements. The figure turned in the mists and moved away. 'Stay! Speak!' Horatio cried after it.

But it was gone. Trembling he stood there. Surely this was something more than fantasy!

And what did it mean? That face, so like the king; so noble, fine and strong in life, now coming to them in death all lacerated with an inward grief. Did it foretell some dreadful menace to the state of Denmark?

He thought then of his friend, Hamlet, the young Prince of Denmark, beloved son of this dead king whose ghost now stalked the battlements. Prince Hamlet must be told of this. Surely the father would bare his sorrows to his son!

This the three men agreed, in solemn secrecy: Prince Hamlet must be told. This very night he would be brought to see this terrifying thing.

◊ ◊ ◊

Even as their minds reeled with the ghost of a king now dead, the new king performed the duties of a monarch with lordly hand in halls a-glitter with celebration. This new king, Claudius, was brother to the king that had just died, and he had cause to celebrate much more than his ascent to the throne of Denmark. Swiftly following his coronation as the king, Claudius had married the dead king's wife. Elsinore was not in mourning for the passing of a king. Instead the gaudy brilliance of velvets, silks and jewels decked out the courtiers who fluttered among silken hangings and heady flowers. Feasting, drinking, music, dance and song trumpeted the gaiety of wedding celebrations. All the world, it seemed, applauded the happy event.

All, that is, except Prince Hamlet. Hamlet loved his father with fierce pride and passion. He loved his mother too. He had thought she was the most loving wife his noble father could have had. How she had hung upon his father's words and deeds, as though she drew her life from his!

But now? That noble father dead: not even two months dead. And this loving wife? This passionate, devoted wife had wed again! Within a month! This wife had wed her husband's brother! Against all the customs of the land that frowned upon a marriage to a husband's brother, called it incest ...

Wed! To a man as foul as Hamlet's father had been glorious. How could the

world applaud it? Hamlet ached with its treachery to his beloved father. He shrank within his dark mourning clothes as if he would melt away, forever escaping these garish, gaudy, rotten halls. He watched the king, his uncle, whose smile was as wide as his broad, bloated face. His hand never left the jewelled fingers of his queen. And Hamlet loathed the ground on which they stood: his whole body was consumed with longing for his father.

'But now my nephew Hamlet and my son,' King Claudius, all glowing smiles, was now approaching him. 'How is it that the clouds still hang on you?'

'Good Hamlet,' his mother urged. 'Cast away your gloom and look like a friend on Claudius.' She smiled luxuriously at her new husband. 'Do not for ever seek your noble father in the dust; you know death is common: all that lives must die ...'

So was a king dismissed, a husband gone! All that lives must die! 'Aye, madam, death is common,' Hamlet answered bitterly.

An impatient sweep of the king's glittering hand interrupted him. 'It is sweet and commendable in your nature, Hamlet, to give these mourning duties to your father. But you must know, your father lost a father; that father lost, lost his. We pray you, cast aside this sorrow, and think of me as of a father.'

The queen tilted her handsome head, and smiled as if she could simply smile away Hamlet's misery.

Emptiness doused the fire of his anger. 'I shall in all my best obey you, madam,' he muttered. He watched them go, this gilded queen and king, wafted by courtiers fluttering like desperate butterflies about an overblown flower. The silence settled about him, a gloom that shut out sunlight. If only he could simply cease to be, end his life now, and so end all the pain.

'Oh, that this too, too solid flesh would melt, thaw and resolve itself into a dew!' he cried into the void around him. 'Oh God! How weary, stale, flat and unprofitable seem to me all the uses of this world. It's an unweeded garden that grows to seed ... things rank and gross in nature possess it!' What a stench and ugliness was in it! In his mind he traced the contours of his father's strong, wise face. 'Only two months dead!' And then with sudden horror he saw his uncle's face, larded with that gleam of cunning. 'A beast would have mourned longer! But break, my heart, for I must hold my tongue!'

A sudden noise behind him: three men approached. And as they neared, a beam of sun broke through his clouds. The man who greeted him was no twittering courtier from Elsinore, but dear Horatio, friend from university in Wittenberg! Here was a man whose honest friendship was as dear to him as any he had ever had!

But why in Elsinore? He grasped Horatio's hand, urging explanation.

'My lord,' Horatio replied unwillingly. 'I came to see your father's funeral.'

Hamlet regarded him with a long, silent look that chilled Horatio as surely as the sight of Hamlet's father's ghost.

'I pray you, do not mock me, fellow-student,' Hamlet said, 'I think it was to see my mother's wedding.'

'Indeed, my lord, it followed hard upon it.' And Horatio told him then, carefully, what they had witnessed on the battlements.

With every word a flame seemed to flicker across Prince Hamlet's face, as though a hidden life was kindling there again.

Then with sudden resolution he said, 'I will watch tonight. Perhaps it will walk again. If it looks like my noble father I'll speak to it, though hell itself should open and bid me hold my peace!'

Warmly he grasped their hands. 'Upon the battlements, between eleven and twelve, I'll visit you.'

His father's spirit! He shivered. This phantom was an echo of the sombre misery within his soul, as though some dreadful knowledge was struggling upward from the kingdom of the dead towards him.

'Foul deeds will rise,' he murmured, 'though all the earth may bury them from men's eyes.'

◇ ◇ ◇

With Hamlet, Horatio and Marcellus waited on the battlements.

'Look!' Horatio murmured, 'Look, my lord, it comes.'

'Angels and ministers of grace defend us!' Hamlet leapt to his feet and stared, finding no other words to pass his trembling lips.

Then he seemed to haul on inner strength and took a step towards the phantom. 'I will speak to you: I'll call you king, father, royal Dane. Oh, answer me! What does this mean?'

The phantom's hand rose through the mists and hovered. It beckoned to Prince Hamlet: once, twice, three times.

As if drawn by an invisible thread, Hamlet moved after it.

'Do not go with it,' Marcellus warned.

'Do not, my lord,' Horatio said, holding Hamlet by the arm.

'Why?' Hamlet cried. 'What should I fear? I'll follow it!'

'Be ruled,' Horatio spoke gently to his friend. 'You shall not go.'

'My fate cries out! Unhand me gentlemen! By heaven I'll make a ghost of him that stops me!' And with a burst of strength Hamlet threw off their hold and rushed into the swirling mists.

Horatio stared after him. He felt the chill of doom across his heart: for Hamlet, and for all of them.

Marcellus said quietly, 'Come, let's follow him. It is not right to leave him alone with this.' And with a shudder of dread, 'Something is rotten in the state of Denmark.'

Father and son stood together, wrapped in the silent blanket of the night and in their lonely grief.

'Mark me,' the apparition gazed with longing across the boundary of death that kept him from his son. 'My hour is almost come.'

'Speak,' Hamlet whispered. 'I am bound to hear.'

'If ever you did love your father,' the spirit's voice welled from the castle stones and echoed in the air, 'revenge his foul and most unnatural murder!'

Murder! The word boomed across the towers and blasted into Hamlet as if it would hurl him in a thousand shattered pieces across the earth.

'Murder!'

'Murder most foul,' the echo of his father's voice tore through his ears.

Murder! But all the world knew that his father died from a serpent's poisoned sting!

'Know now,' the spirit breathed, 'the serpent that did sting your father's life now wears his crown.'

'My uncle!' Numbly Hamlet looked into his father's bloodless face. Numbly he struggled to hear him through the hammering in his brain: how Claudius had crept to where the king slept peacefully in his orchard; how Claudius had poured a poison in his ear that coursed through his veins like quicksilver and soured his life.

But now a new horror crept from the phantom's lips into Hamlet's mind, and held him, stunned: his mother, who had seemed to love his father so, had, even before his father's death, entwined herself with that foul, murderous Claudius' lust.

Hamlet swayed in an agony of shock. A mother steeped in dishonesty and faithlessness even while his father was alive!

'Thus was I, sleeping, by a brother's hand, of life, of crown, of queen, at once dispatched,' the spirit mourned. 'If you have nature in you, do not bear it. Let not the royal bed be a couch for damned incest!'

Now the darkness had begun to pale. The scent of morning spiced the air. With a long, lingering gaze, the spirit studied his son's stricken face. 'Farewell! Farewell! Hamlet, remember me!' And as the dawn crept hesitantly across the hill, the phantom faded. Hamlet was alone.

Remember you! He fought to hold his staggering brain together. He would wipe away all else his memory held and this commandment alone would live within his mind: Revenge his father's foul and most unnatural murder! He recalled his mother's face as she had turned her gaze on smiling Claudius. 'Oh, most vile woman! Oh, villain, villain; smiling, damned villain!' He drew a deep breath. Revenge. He had sworn it. Revenge.

As from a great distance, he heard his friends approaching. He steeled himself to meet their questioning eyes. How could such evil be believed by honest men?

He hailed them now, and swiftly hid his knowledge deep, preparing to fend off their questions.

Already there was the glimmering of a plan inside his head. Swiftly he urged his friends to keep the secret of this night's mysteries. Then he made them swear another, stranger oath: that, however oddly he might behave in times to come, even if he seemed a little mad, they must never, for a moment, hint of any knowledge to explain his acts.

They swore. And with his arms about their shoulders, Hamlet ushered them from the darkness of the towers into the castle. Even as he did, a brooding gloom began to creep across his heart, threatening to ice the flame of vengeance; for what was this world of murder, treachery, adultery, incest and revenge? Not his world. This was not the stuff that he was made of! 'The time is out of joint,' he cried inwardly. 'Oh cursed spite, that ever I was born to set it right!'

◊   ◊   ◊

The Lord Chamberlain in Claudius' Court was Polonius, an elderly gentleman with many years of politics behind him and a high opinion of the wisdom he had learned in such a wily world. The ebb and flow of power, its cut and thrust and counter-thrust was his life-blood; the schemes, manoeuvres, plans and strategies of courtly government were all his daily bread. He had a son, Laertes, a handsome youth with boundless energy and love of all the pleasures in life. He lived in Paris – a fitting place of residence for a man of fashion. Polonius also had a daughter, Ophelia, a gentle, pretty girl of simple, modest nature to whom the world had shown no harshness or cruelty. She felt only a limitless trust and love for those who cared for her: her brother Laertes, her father Polonius – and Prince Hamlet, who had warmly vowed his love for her.

It was true her brother had warned her that she should not take Prince Hamlet's words of love too seriously, for on a prince's choice depended the safety and the health of the whole state. Her father had added his scorn. Surely she, so much beneath a prince's station in life, could not take a prince's words of love as meaning anything! Polonius had smelt a scandal brewing. Ophelia in silly innocence would disgrace herself, and make a pretty fool of him!

'I would not, from this time forth, have you talk with Prince Hamlet,' he had warned her then, wagging his finger in her face, his tone defying any disobedience.

Ophelia had stared at her father's threatening finger in disbelief. Why did they all judge Hamlet's words of love as false? She knew Hamlet, in her heart: an

honest, loving man, who would not trifle with her love.

Yet she knew her brother and her father loved her too, sought only to protect her from all harm. With their understanding of the world, perhaps they did know more of this than she ... And so she had obeyed her father's harsh commandment – sent back Prince Hamlet's letters and denied his visits to her.

Now, two months had passed since that dark night when Hamlet saw his father's ghost upon the battlements. And in that time such change had come upon him! Ophelia, frightened, blurted her horror of it to her father, Polonius. This noble Prince Hamlet, this fine, fine man, his clothes all crumpled and awry, and with a look so pale and pitiful as if he had been loosed out of hell to tell its horror, had come to her room, gazed at her face in misery, sighed piteously ...

The cause was clear to Polonius, his mind racing with what uses he could make of it. Hamlet was mad for Ophelia's love! What news to give the king! This must be the very ecstasy of love, and surely was the source of the madness afflicting the prince these past two months!

King Claudius and his queen already had plans afoot to sniff out the cause of Hamlet's antics in the past two months. Neither his appearance nor the inward man seemed to resemble what it used to be, and even Horatio would shed no light on the reasons for this transformation. Instead, the king had sent for Hamlet's old school friends, Rosencrantz and Guildenstern. Perhaps, he told them, as companions of Hamlet's happy youth, they could find the reason for his melancholy strangeness. The queen added her pleas for help, for Hamlet's continuing unhappiness and growing madness marred the pleasure and the comforts of her luxurious days.

So Rosencrantz and Guildenstern were sent to look for Hamlet and inform the king and queen of all they knew.

Now Polonius bustled in, puffed with pride that he, of all, had found the cause of Hamlet's lunacy. His words spilled like tripping idiots off his tongue.

'To expostulate,' he declared, 'what majesty should be, what duty is, what day is day, night is night and time is time ...'

The queen sighed heavily. How tedious this councillor could be! 'More matter with less art,' she told him.

Polonius bowed, but did not pause in the tumbling gambol of his words. 'Your noble son is mad. Consider,' he gazed about him with pleasure at the effect his next pronouncement would have, 'I have a daughter, who in obedience has given me this,' and with a flourish he took a letter from his robes, reading it aloud with flowing roundness to the words of love, pausing to criticise each phrase so that all his listeners could see his breadth of knowledge, before producing his opinion like a rabbit from a conjuror's hat: 'Lord Hamlet, repulsed, fell into a sadness, then into a weakness, and so into the madness in which he raves and we all mourn for.'

'Do you think it is this?' Claudius asked the queen.

'It may be, very likely,' the queen replied.

Polonius even had a scheme to test the truth of it. Ophelia should meet Hamlet, as if by chance. Polonius and the king could hide nearby and watch how Hamlet behaved to her.

'We will try it,' said Claudius. Each day his misgivings about Prince Hamlet grew. There was no shape to his suspicions, just a pricking sense of danger nearing. And even as they hatched the plot, Prince Hamlet himself approached. Polonius urged the royal pair to go, so he could set an ambush for the prince.

'Do you know me, my lord?' he accosted Hamlet.

Hamlet looked up from his book; a brief, vacant stare, and down again. 'Excellent well, you are a fishmonger,' he said.

'Not I, my lord,' Polonius assured him.

'Then I wish you were so honest a man,' Hamlet retorted.

'Honest, my lord?'

'Aye, sir,' Hamlet replied. 'To be honest, as this world goes, is to be one man picked out of ten thousand.'

'That's very true, my lord,' Polonius said, less certain now of where this conversation might be going.

'Have you a daughter?' Hamlet demanded. 'Let her not walk in the sun.' He eyed Polonius solemnly, and returned to the pages of his book.

Still harping on my daughter! Polonius rejoiced. He said I was a fishmonger. He is far gone, far gone! The old man's eyes grew misty thinking of times long past when he too had suffered for love. 'What do you read, my lord?' he accosted Hamlet again.

'Words, words, words,' Hamlet held the book up.

'What is the matter, my lord?' Polonius persisted.

'Between who?' Hamlet asked.

'I mean the matter that you read, my lord,' explained Polonius, as to a very little child.

'Lies, sir,' replied Hamlet, with a gleam in his eye, 'for the rogue says here that old men have grey beards, that their faces are wrinkled—'

Polonius stepped back. Though this was madness, he could see that there was method in it! He straightened his robes importantly, and bustled out, and Hamlet watched him go.

What a tiresome fool this revered courtier is, he thought; how he deserves to shelter in the murky shadow of King Claudius!

Two men entered the room, two well-known faces from much happier days. 'My excellent good friends!' he exclaimed. 'How do you, Guildenstern? Ah, Rosencrantz! Good lads ...' He shook hands heartily. 'But what have you deserved at the hands of Fortune that she sends you to prison here?'

'Prison, my lord?' exclaimed Guildenstern.

'Denmark's a prison,' Hamlet assured him, 'to me it is a prison.'

'Why then your ambition makes it one,' said Rosencrantz.

Like ice the comment dropped across the easy banter of their words. Hamlet eyed them curiously. Why had they come to Elsinore?

'Were you not sent for?' he questioned. 'Come, deal justly with me; come, come, speak.'

A rising colour in their faces gave a look of guilt. So, he could detect the manipulations of his uncle and his mother in all this!

'My lord,' they admitted uneasily, 'we were sent for.'

'I will tell you why,' Hamlet said, bitterly. 'I have of late lost all my mirth ...'

He turned away as though quite suddenly he lost interest in them. When he looked back, his gaze was harsh.

'What a piece of work is man! How noble in reason! In form and moving how express and admirable! In action how like an angel! In understanding how like a god!' He searched their faces for these glories, and despaired. Yet once he had seen this richness in his fellow men.

His companions laughed a little nervously. Truly this was not the youth they knew! But remembering the orders from the king, Rosencrantz told Hamlet of the actors coming to Elsinore – a theatre company that Hamlet knew well.

Hamlet seemed to shake his gloom away, and already the actors were entering the halls with sparkling swirls of costume. Hamlet greeted old friends enthusiastically, 'Come, give us a taste of your quality,' he urged. 'The rugged Pyrrhus, he whose sable arms ...'

The actors took it up from him, unfolding a tale of vengeance, the sorrow of a widow, Hecuba, across the body of her husband. And Hamlet watched, enthralled, a whirlpool of warring thoughts erupting in his mind, so that on impulse, as the actors left, he stopped one of them. 'Can you play The Murder of Gonzago, and a speech I would insert in it? We'll have it tomorrow night,' he said.

He watched the actor go. His head would burst with the wild turbulence

within! Was it not monstrous that this actor could, in a mere play, so work his passion up that his face grew pale, tears welled in his eyes, yet Hamlet, with such reasons for passion, could say nothing! Two months ago the ghost had come to him! Two months had trickled past and only numbness filled him whenever he thought of it. Am I a coward? He searched in desperation for a reason for the heaviness that bound his heart and brain and stilled all movement towards revenge. Surely there could be no villain more deserving of a bloody death than Claudius! Bloody, bawdy villain! Remorseless, treacherous, lecherous, kindless villain! Everything called him to kill Claudius and draw his mother from the stinking nest in which she lay with him.

Yet still Hamlet had not done it.

Each day entrenched the villain further in the wealth and power seized by the murder of a king.

Yet he, Hamlet, had done nothing.

Once he'd had the glimmering of a plan: madness had been a disguise to buy him time, from which he meant to take revenge. But two months had gone, and still it was not done.

Now, though, the gleam of something new … a thought he'd had, just as the actors left. The play! 'I'll have the actors play something like the murder of my father before my uncle,' he told himself. 'I'll observe his looks. If he but flinches, I know my course.' Perhaps then this crippling numbness would lift and he could do what must be done. 'The play's the thing,' he assured himself again, 'wherein I'll catch the conscience of the king.'

◇ ◇ ◇

Rosencrantz and Guildenstern could throw no light on Hamlet's madness. So now Ophelia was set to draw it out, and even the queen banished so that Claudius and Polonius could hide alone and watch Ophelia's meeting with the prince. The queen went willingly, thinking how pleasant it would be if Ophelia were the cause of Hamlet's ills, for then her virtues could bring him to his usual self again!

Polonius pushed Ophelia into the hall. So it was that the young girl was abandoned there, while Claudius and Polonius lurked behind a nearby curtain. She was bewildered, and uncertain of the part she was to play. Yet with a kind of desperation she hoped that someone would confirm the cause of Hamlet's illness and find a cure for him.

Ignorant of the hidden watchers, and of Ophelia's shy figure in the shadows, Hamlet wandered by. The certainties that had held him as he planned the play had faded. A vast desolation welled in him again, as though he floated without substance through the world.

If only he could simply cease! 'To be, or not to be, that is the question,' he told himself. 'To die; to sleep,' his mind sniffed after the thought as would a dog along a trail; 'To die, to sleep, perhaps to dream ... Aye there's the obstacle, for in that sleep of death what dreams may come!' A flutter of movement caught his eye: he thrust the privacy of thought away, and turned.

'Good my lord,' Ophelia faltered, looking unwillingly into his face. 'How does your honour for this many a day?'

'I humbly thank you, well, well, well,' he answered, seeing the flare of colour in her face, the nervous glances that she threw about her. Once he had trusted this girl's soft innocence, and loved her well for it. Now he wondered. Was she another trap for him, like Rosencrantz and Guildenstern? Was this frail beauty that he loved a thing of falseness, treachery and ugliness, like his mother?

He pulled the cloak of his madness round him and stared through its mask at her. 'Are you honest?' he demanded.

'My lord?' Ophelia stammered.

Then, as though a curtain lifted from his face, his eyes softened. 'I did love you once,' he murmured.

'Indeed, my lord, you made me believe so,' she said.

Believe! What was belief? He had believed his mother so adored his father that she would die without his life to give her strength. 'You should not have believed me, I loved you not,' he turned from Ophelia, who had become a thing of falseness like his mother.

'I was the more deceived,' faltered Ophelia.

New suspicions leapt to his mind. 'Where's your father?'

The question whipped across Ophelia's shrinking heart. If he discovered that her father and the king lurked near!

'At home, my lord,' she whispered in shame. She felt she would drown in the despair sweeping over her. His breath was hot against her face, and opening her eyes she winced beneath a gaze of such contempt as she had never seen before.

'I say we will have no more marriage! Those that are married already,' Hamlet looked towards the curtain that shielded the secret watchers, 'all but one shall live.' He looked back at her stricken face, as though a ray of warmth still tried to penetrate the hatred in his words. But in a moment it was gone, and so was he.

Claudius swooped with Polonius from their spying place. 'Love!' scorned Claudius, 'his affections do not that way tend. Nor what he spoke, though it lacked form a little, it was not like madness.'

No, there was something else to this: all his instincts told him there was more than Hamlet wanted them to know. Claudius' ready sense of danger warned that the menace drew nearer by the hour.

'He shall be sent with speed to England,' he told Polonius. Might not the sight of seas and other countries dispel his mood? At all costs, Prince Hamlet must be removed from Elsinore.

Polonius, however, was still certain that the prince was mad only for Ophelia's love. Just one more scheme to test the matter out! This time the queen as bait, Polonius placed, of course, to hear their private conversation ...

◇ ◇ ◇

Hamlet also prepared his plan with care. He coached the actors with the words he'd written. With restless excitement he sought Horatio.

'There is a play tonight before the king,' he told him. 'One scene of it comes near the events which I have told you of my father's death. Observe my uncle. If his guilt does not reveal itself, it is an evil ghost that we have seen!'

Aghast at what he heard, Horatio agreed. At all costs this matter must, once and for all, be set to rights.

◇ ◇ ◇

The time had come. All came to watch the play: the king and queen, Polonius and Ophelia, Rosencrantz and Guildenstern and a hundred shining courtiers floating in with rustlings and murmurings and silken, painted smiles. Hamlet greeted all with witty jokes that danced a flippant jig about them. The king thrust off his quips with irritable looks.

'Come here, my dear Hamlet, sit by me,' the queen tried to calm her excited son.

'No, good mother, here's metal more attractive,' he said, turning to Ophelia. She sat with downcast eyes, her face a patchwork of misery.

'You are merry, my lord,' she answered Hamlet's bawdy humour.

'What should a man do but be merry, for look you, how cheerfully my mother looks, and my father died within these two hours!'

'No,' said Ophelia, gently now, 'it is twice two months, my Lord.'

'So long!' said Hamlet. 'Oh heavens, die two months ago and not forgotten yet! Then there's hope a great man's memory may outlive his life half a year!'

But now the lights were dimmed. Music played. The murmurs of the shimmering audience died away. King and queen began to smile expectantly.

Two actors came before them, dressed as king and queen. They began a mime: the queen showed her vast love for the king. The king lay down to sleep. The queen went out. A man crept in, and poured a deadly poison in the sleeping monarch's ear. The queen returned, wildly lamenting the king's death. The poisoner returned and joined her show of grief. The dead king's body was carried away. The poisoner wooed the queen with gifts. At first unwilling, she at last accepted them.

The royal pair and all the gilded courtiers watched the mime. Hamlet and Horatio watched King Claudius. His smile had frozen on his face.

The mime had ended, and now the play began again, this time with words. The player queen protested to the player king how she would love him for ever and never wed again, should ever he lie dead.

'Madam, how do you like this play?' Hamlet asked his mother.

Comfortably, the queen replied, 'The lady does protest too much, I think.'

'Aye, but she'll keep her word,' Hamlet assured her knowingly.

Claudius' smile was now a wound across his face that would not close.

The poisoner came in. He leaned across the sleeping king to pour the poison in his ear.

Hamlet could contain his wild excitement no more. 'He poisons him in the garden for his crown. You shall see how the murderer gets the dead king's wife—'

The gash across Claudius' face opened to a roar.

'Give me some light!' he bellowed, and swept away, and with a crash of fallen chairs the courtiers scuttled in his wake.

◇ ◇ ◇

'Did you perceive?' Hamlet asked Horatio. 'Upon the talk of poisoning?'

'Very well, my lord,' replied Horatio. The king had truly fled before the sight of his own deeds!

But now came Rosencrantz and Guildenstern again, with royal messages: the king was furious and the queen demanded to see Hamlet in her room. Hamlet watched his old school friends running errands for king and queen. Their partnership with his corrupted mother and her damned husband had once made him a little sad. Now it angered him with searing pain. So many people playing games, circling about him like hunters round an animal in a trap!

He gestured them away, for he had done with friends like this. He stood alone.

'It is now the very witching time of night,' he breathed. 'Now could I drink hot blood and do such bitter business as the day would quake to look upon.' He strove to calm his racing thoughts. Softly: now to his mother. But he must not hurt her. 'I will speak daggers to her, but use none,' he told himself.

◇ ◇ ◇

The king was deep in conference with Rosencrantz and Guildenstern. This play had been no casual accident. Hamlet was playing with him, and the scent of danger in Claudius' nostrils was sour.

'It is not safe to let his madness rage,' he argued. 'He shall go now to England along with you. Such dangers as are threatened by his lunacies should not be left to roam so close to the throne of Denmark.'

With only half an ear he heard Polonius say that Hamlet was going to his mother's room, to which Polonius too would hurry, there to hide and hear their conversation. Claudius had other matters on his mind. That play! How foul his acts had looked, grimacing at him from those mouths and eyes! For the first time he saw the deed as others would see it.

'Oh, my offence is rank! It smells to heaven! A brother's murder!' Perhaps he should ask forgiveness from God? 'But what form of prayer? Forgive me my foul murder? That cannot be, since I still have those things for which I did the murder: my crown, my ambition and my queen. Can one be pardoned and still keep the things for which one has sinned?' Perhaps in a house of God he might find praying easier. He entered the castle chapel. 'Help, angels!' He forced his knees to bend. Perhaps if he prayed here, he would be safe.

And so he knelt. As he did, the source of all his terrors came behind him. Hamlet, passing to his mother's room, saw the kneeling figure of his enemy, his broad back offered like a sacrifice to any ready sword, and quickly he drew his own. 'Now might I do it, pat. Now while he is praying.' The sword trembled as he raised it. 'And now I'll do it.'

The weapon hovered and still it did not fall. 'And so he goes to heaven and so am I revenged?' The sword fell, unused, to his side. Despair flowed bleakly through him. Kill Claudius while he prayed? No, that must not be. 'Kill him while he is drunk, or in the incestuous pleasures of his bed, that would be a fitting death for such a man.'

He backed away, sheathing his sword, still arguing within himself. Kill, kill, revenge, the hammer drove on through his brain.

And somewhere beyond the circling arguments he knew so well, there was the single rhythm that he really heard. His father was not revenged. Hamlet had not done it.

◊ ◊ ◊

In her bedroom he faced the queen. 'Now, mother, what's the matter?'

'Hamlet, you have much offended your father,' his mother said.

'Mother, you have much offended my father,' Hamlet retorted.

She coloured, and her comfortable serenity was distorted by a look of unaccustomed anger.

'Have you forgotten who I am?' she demanded.

'No, not so. You are the queen, your husband's brother's wife: and, would it were not so, you are my mother.' He grasped her arm in sudden rage. 'You do not go,' he hissed, 'until I set up a mirror where you may see the inmost part of you.'

In sudden fear the queen drew back. 'Will you murder me? Help!'

Behind the curtain, the listening Polonius yelped.

'How now!' cried Hamlet, drawing his sword. 'A rat? Dead!' He thrust his sword into the curtain.

'What have you done?' gasped the queen.

'I do not know,' Hamlet stared at the blood staining his sword. A wild hope seized him, 'Is it the king?'

'Oh, what a rash and bloody deed is this,' the queen was sobbing, knowing it was the wily councillor Hamlet had killed.

'A bloody deed!' snorted Hamlet. 'Almost as bad, good mother, as kill a king and marry with his brother!'

Kill a king! The queen could not imagine such a thing.

Hamlet twitched back the curtain to see the body. Hope died in him. He let the curtain drop. 'Peace,' he hushed his mother. 'Sit you down, and let me wring your heart.'

'What have I done, that you dare wag your tongue in noise so rude against me?' pleaded the queen.

He showed his father's portrait on a chain around his neck. 'Look here. This was your husband. Look you now what follows,' he seized the portrait of Claudius that stood by his mother's bed. 'Here is your husband: like a mildewed ear blasting his wholesome brother. Have you eyes? You cannot call it love!'

'Oh, Hamlet, speak no more,' begged his mother. 'You turn my eyes into my very soul and there I see such black and grained spots ...'

'But to live in the rank sweat of his bed, stewed in corruption, honeying and making love over the nasty sty like pigs—' Hamlet pleaded with her.

'These words like daggers enter my ears. No more, sweet Hamlet!' she

entreated him. 'You tear my heart in two!'

'Throw away the worser part of it and live the purer with the other half,' he urged her. 'Go not to my uncle's bed.' He searched her face for signs of honesty. 'I must go to England, you know that?' he asked.

The queen sighed heavily. 'I had forgotten.'

'And my two schoolfellows, whom I will trust as I would trust fanged adders, will sweep me on my way.'

His mother watched him go, dragging the body of Polonius. Her love for him warred with horror at the madness she suspected in her son's wild brain; and yet below it all there was a throbbing guilt that told her, in her innermost heart, that Prince Hamlet was not mad and spoke only the truth.

◇ ◇ ◇

News of Polonius' death pierced through the king like a swordthrust to his heart. How close the danger came! Hamlet must be sent to England with all speed! He was now a prisoner. And in the hands of Rosencrantz and Guildenstern, Claudius had entrusted letters, sealed and directed to the King of England. They asked that, on arrival on England's shores, Hamlet be put to death.

Hamlet, close-guarded by Rosencrantz and Guildenstern, travelled towards his ship, and death, in England. So it came about that he stood high up on a hill, and looked down at the army of Prince Fortinbras of Norway moving across Denmark's plains, towards war in Poland. Here was yet another show of others' speed and strength and will to act! Here twenty thousand men marched to war, led by a prince of steel who did not flinch from any task before him!

'I do not know why yet I live to say "this thing's to be done,"' Hamlet ached with self-loathing and disgust. 'I that have a father killed, a mother stained ... And yet I let all sleep. Oh, from this time forth,' he told himself for perhaps the hundredth time, 'my thoughts be bloody or be nothing worth!'

◇ ◇ ◇

The fragile Ophelia was floundering in the mire of Elsinore, and knew that she was drowning. So fast the blows beat down on her! Severed from Hamlet by her father's hand, bewildered by the plots and counterplots, savaged by Hamlet's scorn of her, her misery had stretched to breaking point. Now her father dead, killed by the man she loved.

Her frail nature snapped, like a flowering branch caught in a storm, blossoms torn and trampled on the ground. Whispering strange snatches of bawdy songs, she wandered lonely in the castle halls; told of tricks and plots, sighed, laughed, always alone.

The courtiers whispered of her tragedy. They whispered too about her brother, for Laertes had learned of his father's death and had returned, hot-foot from France.

Claudius prepared. Steadily he turned Laertes' rage towards Prince Hamlet. The wasted figure of Ophelia drifted by, no recognition of her brother on her face, a scrap of song upon her lips, arms laden with imagined gifts of flowers which she bestowed with gentle grace on everyone she saw. She sang of violets withering when her father died, of death and tombs and graves.

Claudius watched Laertes. He was burning now with more than rage at his father's death; here were a sister's wasted wits to be revenged! Claudius gave a thousand reasons why he had not moved against Prince Hamlet openly: the queen so loved her son; the people loved him too and would not easily see him accused of murder. He did not give the most important reason of all, that he feared what Hamlet, on trial, might say about the murder of a king!

Then came the news that spiked their musings into daggers and awoke old terrors in Claudius. Hamlet was not on board the ship approaching England and his death! He was again in Denmark.

Claudius sharpened his ready wits to cunning. 'What would you undertake against this murderer to show yourself your father's son in deed more than in words?' he asked Laertes.

The young man's face flamed with vicious anger. 'To cut his throat in the church!'

Here was the man to kill the prince! It must be done, thought Claudius, in such a way that people saw it was an accident. Laertes – so much a son of his old wily father – saw no dishonour in catching their prey by devious means and

hidden murder. The plot was laid: a fencing match between Hamlet and Laertes – a swordfight for sport to match their skills against each other. Hamlet, Claudius assured Laertes, was too trusting a man to check the weapons. He would not know that Laertes used a blade without a button to cover its deadly point. Nor would he know that Laertes' blade was poisoned, the slightest scratch bringing instant death to Hamlet. Nor that the king would have ready a poisoned cup ... This time there would be no escape from death for Hamlet.

◇   ◇   ◇

There was a churchyard close beside the towers of Elsinore, and here two gravediggers dug a grave. Here, the poor battered frame of frail Ophelia would be laid, at last, to rest.

Clambering to hang garlands of wild flowers on the weeping branches of a willow tree, she had fallen to the brook below, and floated there, cushioned on her billowing skirts, chanting wistful snatches of old tunes, until her sodden garments pulled her to her muddy, lonely death. So had Ophelia finally escaped Elsinore.

Much used to the grim task of making holes for dead people to lie in, the gravediggers chattered and joked about their work as would any workman wiling away a long and weary day. In this jovial mood they little noticed the two men who came upon their merriment and watched them curiously: Horatio and Hamlet on their way from seashore to Elsinore, Hamlet telling all that had happened since he set sail.

What a turn of fate there had been! From the moment he had boarded the ship some instinct had told him there was new devilry afoot. Secretly, by night, he had taken the letters carried by Rosencrantz and Guildenstern. There he had read Claudius' order for his death in England. No sooner had he discovered this than they had been attacked by pirates; Hamlet, leaping aboard the pirate ship, was taken prisoner, while his own ship broke free and swept on its way to England. Rosencrantz and Guildenstern, these messengers of death, now carried letters, written and sealed by Hamlet, requesting that the bearers of the letters be put to instant death!

'So Guildenstern and Rosencrantz go to it,' Horatio murmured, awestruck at their fate.

'Why, they did make love to this employment!' Hamlet swept this aside. 'They are not near my conscience.' But the pirates had dealt fairly with him, and agreed to leave him on Denmark's shores.

So back to Elsinore, and to his uncle. But now the self-disgust with which he'd watched the massing armies of Prince Fortinbras had been fired by the events at sea to a kind of recklessness, a drive to ride the current of fate wherever it carried him.

Horatio put a quieting hand upon his arm: a train of mourners was drawing near, bearing the body of a girl. Hamlet looked up. A flame shot through him, a memory of almost buried love, a look of her as he had seen her last. 'The fair Ophelia!' he whispered.

'Sweets to the sweet: farewell!' his mother's mournful tones reached his ears. She scattered flowers across Ophelia. 'I hoped you would have been my Hamlet's wife.'

Unshed tears pricked Hamlet's eyes, the crowding misery of guilt, the understanding of how wrongly he had savaged her. He saw Laertes leap into the grave and take his sister's body in his arms. How dare they mouth of sorrows, grief and loss, these kings and queens and courtiers who used people as playthings for their needs! He charged blindly forwards, and with a cry of, 'This is I, Hamlet the Dane,' he leapt into the grave, defying one and all to match his anguish.

'The devil take your soul,' Laertes yelled, and flew at him.

'Pluck them apart,' bellowed the king. The two were hauled from the grave, and Hamlet faced Laertes.

'I loved Ophelia!' he cried. 'Forty thousand brothers could not with all their quantity of love make up my sum. Will you weep? Will you fight? Will you eat crocodile? I'll do it! Do you come here to outface me with leaping in her grave? Be buried now with her and so will I!'

King Claudius watched them both with narrowed eyes. Now quickly to this fencing match: no delay. Only Hamlet's certain death would suit his purposes.

◇ ◇ ◇

In quieter mood Hamlet reflected on Laertes' rage, and how the world had dealt sore blows to this young man. A father killed (by Hamlet's own hand), a sister maddened and dead: it seemed to Hamlet now that it was the mirror portrait of his own misery, and he regretted his own anger in the grave. So he accepted the fencing match offered by King Claudius to settle the hot blood between him and Laertes in honourable fashion.

For a moment a shifting unease moved deep within him, like a stirring from the rottenness of Elsinore. But he pushed it aside.

'If your mind dislikes anything, obey it,' Horatio pressed him.

'Not a whit!' said Hamlet. 'There's special fate in the fall of a sparrow. If it is now, it is not to come. If it is not to come, it will be now. If it is not now, yet it will come: the readiness is all!'

◇ ◇ ◇

The time had come. The courtiers came to watch the fencing match.

'Give me your pardon, sir; I have done you wrong,' Prince Hamlet said to Polonius' son.

Laertes received the apology courteously enough, but still insisted that they satisfy their honour with the match.

Hamlet gestured towards the weapons, 'Give us the swords.'

'This is too heavy,' Laertes said, 'let me see another.' He picked up the unprotected, poisoned blade.

'Are they all the same length?' asked Hamlet, and chose one casually, making

passes through the air with it to feel its weight and balance.

King Claudius called for wine. 'The king drinks to Hamlet,' he said, and held the cup aloft. 'In the cup I will throw this pearl ...' Claudius held high his master-stroke, the pearl of secret poison.

The fencing bout began. Hamlet and Laertes circled warily, weapons nosing out the other's speed and skill with thrust and counter-thrust.

And then with cat-like leap and whip-like blade, Hamlet lunged and caught Laertes.

'A hit,' the cry rose from the courtiers.

Now, the king dropped the pearl of death into the cup. 'Give him the cup,' he ordered with a benevolent smile.

'I'll play this bout first,' said Hamlet.

The second bout began. 'Another hit, what say you?' Hamlet panted.

'A touch, a touch, I do confess,' Laertes said. He seemed, the audience noticed, to be holding back, as though he waited for a moment yet to come.

'Here, Hamlet, take my napkin and rub your brow,' said the queen. 'The queen drinks to your fortune, Hamlet.' She lifted the poisoned cup.

'Do not drink!' the king rose to his feet in shock.

'I will, my lord,' the queen smiled at him, playfully defiant, and raised the poisoned cup. She took a long, luxurious drink from it.

Claudius sank to his seat. 'It is too late!'

And in a dream of horror he saw Laertes' poisoned blade dart out and pierce

the prince's side. He saw the prince stare down at trickling blood.

A sudden understanding flared in Hamlet. This was no sport! This was a fight for life! With a great yell of fury he sprang at Laertes, wrestling the poisoned blade away. And with the weapon in his hands, he pierced the arm of Polonius' treacherous son.

The queen stood up, staggered towards her son, and fell.

Hamlet swayed. A lightness had overcome his limbs. 'How is the queen?' he panted.

'She faints to see them bleed,' Claudius croaked in panic.

'No, no, the drink. Oh, my dear Hamlet, I am poisoned,' the queen cried, and fell back, dead.

'Villainy!' cried Hamlet. 'Let the door be locked! Treachery, seek it out!'

'It is here, Hamlet; Hamlet you are killed.' Laertes raised himself in twisting agony, and pointed to the poisoned sword. From lips already paling in death, he poured out the tale of treachery.

Hamlet held Laertes' sword. He looked at the king. Claudius rose in terror. The drumming in Hamlet's brain reached a crescendo, and with a shout of pent-up rage and hate he rushed at the shrinking figure of the king and thrust the blade deep into him. 'Here you incestuous, murderous, damned Dane. Drink your potion! Follow my mother!' and he forced the poisoned cup between the trembling lips.

Hamlet stumbled back into Horatio's arms. A vast void was swallowing him. The sound of marching feet rang through the castle halls. 'What warlike noise is this?' he breathed; struggling to lift his head. It was young Fortinbras, the prince of steel, returning from his wars in Poland and coming to Elsinore, victorious.

Hamlet fell back, and closed his eyes. 'I die, Horatio. The potent poison overwhelms my spirit. But I do prophesy the throne of Denmark will fall on Fortinbras. He has my dying vote: so tell him.' He breathed a deep shuddering sigh. 'The rest is silence.'

Horatio held the crumpled body of his friend. 'Now cracks a noble heart,' he whispered. 'Good night, sweet prince, and flights of angels sing you to your rest.'

And so Prince Fortinbras came upon the havoc of death that strewed the halls of Elsinore. He stood in awe before the desolate sight. A king, a queen, a prince, a courtier all dead. Here was a tale to chill the marrow of the bravest soldier's bones! He heard the tragic story of the Prince of Denmark from loyal Horatio's lips.

Then he raised his head and looked around the devastation that was Elsinore. 'Let four captains bear Hamlet, like a soldier, to the stage,' he said. 'Let the soldiers' music and the rites of war speak loudly for him! He was likely, had he lived, to have proved most royal ...'

◇ ◇ ◇

ANTONY

AND

CLEOPATRA

YEARS HAD PASSED SINCE the bloody battlefield where Mark Antony and Octavius Caesar had avenged the murder of Julius Caesar. Now, with Lepidus, they ruled the Roman world. From its heart in Rome the arms of their power stretched to every corner of the ancient world.

But Mark Antony was not in Rome. Nor was he ranging the far-flung corners of the empire with his army. He was in Egypt. This mighty ruler of the ancient world had turned his back on calls of duty from Rome, and in the luxury of Alexandria he romped in love-games with a playful queen. He had become, so people said, the bellows and the fan to cool a gipsy's lust! Cleopatra, Queen of Egypt, claimed the mind and heart of Antony.

Wrapped in her arms, Mark Antony was annoyed by the messengers from Rome. They brought the breath of urgency, the severe demands of public duty, like an icy blast across the idleness of love-locked days. They almost glowered at him with the disapproving brows of Octavius Caesar himself.

'Nay, hear them, Antony,' teased Cleopatra. Perhaps, she taunted, his abandoned wife, Fulvia, was angry, or youthful Caesar had sent his powerful mandate to him.

'Let Rome in the River Tiber melt, and the wide arch of the empire fall!' Antony dismissed the Roman Empire, Octavius and all, and clasped the laughing Cleopatra to him. 'Here is my space! The nobleness of life is to do thus.' He kissed her with the long, searching kiss of passion.

'Hear the ambassadors,' said Cleopatra, stemming the tide of words with kisses.

Antony refused. 'Speak not to us!' he warned Octavius' messengers, and was lost once more to the demanding eyes of Rome, plunged into the vast pleasure-garden of his love with Cleopatra.

It did not last. In the midst of that night's mirth, Antony abruptly left the festivities, and Cleopatra knew he thought of Rome. She went in search of him. She saw him moving along the corridor with Rome's ambassador. The threat of his departure dropped like a chill shroud about her and instantly she chose to punish him.

'We will not look upon him,' she announced, and swept away.

Antony had consented, finally, to hear the news from Rome. In an instant the grim rhythm of the world outside these walls gripped him like a vice: his wife, Fulvia, had gone to war against his brother, Lucius. Still discontented, she then joined forces with Lucius, and together they'd made war on Octavius Caesar, met defeat and been driven out of Italy.

And Antony? Where was Antony, this all-powerful general of the Roman world? Antony saw the unspoken question in the ambassador's face, and felt Cleopatra's web of love drag at him like a prison's chains. 'These strong Egyptian fetters I must break,' he breathed, 'or lose myself.'

There was more news: his wife Fulvia was dead. It brought no sorrow with it. Antony had long desired to be free of her: his heart had room only for Cleopatra. But thoughts of Rome again broke through the all-consuming image of his love. 'I must with haste leave here,' he repeated his decision to his friend and fellow soldier, Enobarbus.

'Cleopatra, catching but the least noise of this, dies instantly,' Enobarbus told him dryly. 'I have seen her die twenty times upon far poorer reasons!'

'No more light answers,' Antony rebuked him. The call from Rome rang loudly in his ears: too many letters begged for his immediate return. The empire under threat: no less than civil war was looming! Eight years ago there had been civil war when Julius Caesar fought the rival general Pompey and defeated him. Now the youngest son of Pompey rode inward on the tide of his dead father's fame to challenge for the rule of Rome itself. Already this Pompey commanded the empire of the sea. His support on land grew daily among those who did not thrive beneath the triumvir rule of Octavius, Antony and Lepidus.

'Let our officers have notice of what we intend,' Antony commanded Enobarbus. 'I shall break the cause of our urgency to the queen, and get her permission to depart ...'

◊ ◊ ◊

'Where is he?' Cleopatra asked her attendant, Charmian. 'See where he is and who's with him,' she told another, then hastily called him back. 'I did not send you,' she reminded him to play his part with care. 'If you find him sad, say I am dancing; if in mirth, report that I am sudden sick: quick, and return!' And seeing Antony approaching she threw a hasty faint into Charmian's arms. 'Help me away, dear Charmian, I shall fall ... Pray you, stand further from me,' she instructed Antony haughtily.

'What's the matter?' Antony asked, bewildered. He had come with news of

Fulvia's death and reasons for his return to Rome, but already they were fleeing from his tongue.

'What says the married woman?' demanded Cleopatra. But she gave him no chance to speak, for she was balanced precariously between terror that he would go to Fulvia, and anger that he even dared to think of it. 'Never was there a queen so mightily betrayed!'

'Cleopatra ...' protested Antony.

'Why should I think you can be mine and true, who have been false to Fulvia?' she raged.

'Most sweet queen ...' he tried to show the letter in his hand.

'Bid farewell, and go,' she cried. 'When you begged to stay, then was the time for words ... Eternity was in my lips and eyes, bliss in my brows' curve ...'

'Hear me, queen,' yelled Antony and, in a great rush of words, he told her: civil war in Italy; support for Pompey growing daily ...

Last, he produced the reason which should remove all Cleopatra's terror at his return to Rome: his wife was dead.

'Can Fulvia die?' Cleopatra asked suspiciously. She eyed him, and in a moment a new torrent of accusations flooded over him: so this was how her own death would be greeted, with no sorrow, not a single tear!

Buffeted by the storms of passion conjured in an instant by the queen, Antony was lost in the bewildering maze of Cleopatra's changes. Only when the storm was over, did he try again.

'I'll leave you, lady,' he said, awkward in his determination.

She heard him, and she stopped. He turned away. In that instant she understood he truly meant to leave.

And in that moment, Cleopatra, too, was tongue-tied. 'Courteous lord, one word,' she began. 'Sir, you and I must part ...' she faltered, 'but that's not it.' She began again. 'Sir, you and I have loved ... but there's not it ...' She lapsed into silence, words vanishing before the understanding that the man she loved was leaving and she was powerless to stop him.

Finally, elaborately, she sighed. She murmured, 'Your honour calls you away, therefore be deaf to my unpitied folly, and all the gods go with you! Upon your sword sit laurel victory! And smooth success be strewed before your feet!'

Antony took her hand. 'Come,' he encouraged her, gently now. 'Our separation will so fly that you, residing here, go with me, and I fleeing away, remain here with you ...'

◇ ◇ ◇

In Rome, Octavius waited for Antony's return angrily, and every hour the streets of Rome rang louder with news of Pompey's rising fortunes. 'Let Antony's shames quickly drive him to Rome,' muttered Caesar. He turned to Lepidus. 'It is time we two showed ourselves in the battlefield. Pompey thrives in our idleness!'

In Alexandria, Cleopatra plunged into a living death. 'Oh, that I might sleep out this great gap of time my Antony is away,' she sighed to Charmian. 'Where do you think that he is now? Does he stand, or sit? Or does he walk? Or is he on a horse?' She clutched at messages from him, relived each moment of their delivery with cries of admiration, tears of joy and wails of sorrow, while messengers from her to Antony flew thick after him.

In Sicily, seat of his power, young Pompey's confidence grew daily. Already his fleets controlled the sea, for two powerful pirates were his allies. He contemplated with some pleasure the image of Mark Antony in Egypt, sodden in a field of feasts and drink that kept his brain fuming and his body tied in love with Cleopatra.

The news that Antony was not in Egypt but was expected every hour in Rome struck a note of startled fear in him. Mark Antony's skills as a soldier and general were twice those of Lepidus and Octavius Caesar together. But, Pompey consoled himself, there was triumph also in the fact that his challenge to the triumvirs was enough to pluck Antony from Cleopatra's sumptuous arms.

◇ ◇ ◇

Octavius Caesar and Mark Antony eyed each other warily. Nervously, ageing Lepidus watched them both. They had not met, these three pillars of the Roman world, since Antony went to Egypt. Grievances had festered – the wars by Antony's wife and brother against Octavius; Antony's refusal to hear Octavius' messengers or answer calls for help.

Octavius voiced the accusations, one by one, and grimly glared at Antony's too-casual replies. And, desperately watching, Enobarbus and Caesar's advisers looked for a way to bind the alliance tight again against the looming civil war that threatened all of them.

Agrippa, from Caesar's side, reminded them: with his wife Fulvia's death, Antony was free to marry. Let him take Caesar's sister, Octavia, as wife, and so bind the political alliance with Caesar with a brother's loyalties!

There was a fascinated silence. All eyes turned on Antony, so newly sprung from the arms of Egypt's passionate queen. Known for his all-consuming love of her!

Antony measured the proposal. Far from Cleopatra's fervent call, this urgent cry for unity against the swords of civil war rang louder in his ears. He acknowledged its insistent, warning rhythm. To Octavius he said, 'Let me have your hand, and from this hour the heart of brothers govern our loves and sway our great designs!'

'There is my hand,' Octavius Caesar answered him. A cautious gleam of welcome to the pact softened, for a moment, the dark glitter of his eye.

'A sister I bequeath you, whom no brother did ever love so dearly: let her live to join our kingdoms and our hearts; and never fly off our loves again!'

'Happily, amen!' applauded Lepidus. And swiftly all retired to prepare the marriage and their war against young Pompey.

Behind the departing backs of the triumvirs, Enobarbus shook his head. Though whether with regret or disapproval or relief, or merely plain amazement, no one could have told. And his old friends Mecaenas

and Agrippa were more interested to hear him tell of Egypt's wonders than to digest the marvels that had just passed here.

'Eight wild-boars roasted whole at breakfast, and but twelve persons there; is this true?' Mecaenas enquired wonderingly.

'This was but as a fly by an eagle,' Enorbarbus assured him, 'we had much more monstrous matters of feast ...'

'She is a most triumphant lady, if report be square to her,' Mecaenas said.

Enobarbus thought of the absent queen whose presence reached across the world, even to this room. 'When she first met Mark Antony, she pursed up his heart, upon the river of Cydnus!' he laughed to remember it, searching for words that could encompass the glory of that unforgotten moment. 'The barge she sat in, like a burnished throne, burned on the water: the poop was beaten gold, purple the sails, and so perfumed that the winds were love-sick with them; the oars were silver, which to the tune of flutes kept stroke ...' and for the moment, even Enobarbus was transported by the memory.

His listeners, understanding, said with disbelief, 'Now Antony must leave her utterly!'

'Never.' Enobarbus' tone was absolute. 'He will not. Age cannot wither her, nor custom stale her infinite variety ...'

'If beauty, wisdom, modesty, can settle the heart of Antony, Octavia is a blessed prize to him,' Mecaenas assured Enobarbus.

Enobarbus only looked at them with some amusement. They did not know Cleopatra; nor, it seemed, did they know Antony.

◇ ◇ ◇

In Rome, Antony married Octavia, and
promised to keep faith with her. But
even as the echo of his words was
fading, he confessed to himself, 'I will
go to Egypt.' Already the calls to Roman
duty were fading coldly beside the call to
Cleopatra's love. 'I will go to Egypt. And
though I make this marriage for my
peace, in the east my pleasure lies ...'

◇ ◇ ◇

And so they went to meet young
Pompey's challenge: Mark Antony,
Octavius Caesar, and the ageing Lepidus
– their armies gathered and their powers
as one.

Waiting in Alexandria, Cleopatra
smouldered for absent Antony, filled up
her days with memories of him, seized
on every messenger that came from him
as though they brought life again to one
who waned for wanting.

With the same ecstasy she greeted the messenger who brought a different
news. She saw at once he nursed a miserable burden. Terror that Antony was dead
seared through her. But this denied, she paced frantically before the hapless
messenger, filling the air with words to block the news she feared.

'Good madam, hear me,' he protested.

'Well, go to, I will,' she said, but moved immediately to stare with narrowed
eyes at him, 'but there's no goodness in your face! I have a mind to strike you
before you speak. Yet, if you say that Antony lives, is well, or friends with Caesar,
I'll set you in a shower of gold and hail rich pearls upon you ...'

'Madam, he's well,' the messenger broke in.

'Well said,' said Cleopatra.

'And friends with Caesar,' he continued.

'You are an honest man,' she told him happily.

'But yet, madam ...'

She swung round and glared. 'I do not like "but yet,"' she hissed.

Throwing all care to the winds, the messenger gulped out the news, 'Madam ... he's married to Octavia!'

Cleopatra stared, uncomprehending. Then understanding stabbed her with such fury that her hand flew up and struck the messenger, before he or anyone had understood the violence that tore through the shaking queen.

'Horrible villain!' she spat the words at him. 'I'll spurn your eyes like balls before me: you shall be whipped with wire, and stewed in brine, smarting in lingering pickle!'

'Gracious madam,' the messenger protested, trying to escape her flaying hands, 'I that do bring the news did not make the match!'

'Say it is not so,' she yelled. 'A province I will give you!'

'He's married, madam,' stoutly the messenger repeated, and for his pains was forced to leap from the blade of a murderous knife.

'Rogue, you have lived too long,' the hysterical queen was shrieking. 'Melt Egypt into Nile! and kindly creatures turn to serpents ...' she sobbed, and fell on Charmian.

◇ ◇ ◇

The sparring Roman parties met to talk before they went to war: Pompey with his pirate allies against the Roman triumvirs. Fronting power to power, they bargained for a settlement to tie up Pompey's discontented sword and buy peace. To Pompey, the triumvirs offered the island realms of Sicily and Sardinia; in return, they asked that he would rid the seas of pirates and send shipments of grain to Rome.

Pompey, facing the powers of all three triumvirs combined, found the proffered peace bargain more attractive – for the moment.

So it was agreed. The order of the day became not bloodshed, butchery and death, but celebration to hail a pact of peace. On Pompey's ship, anchored off the coast of Italy, these leaders of the Roman world and the would-be contender for their power met. These who might have been engaged in hacking off each other's limbs, gathered instead to shake each other's hands, embrace as friends and taste together the pleasures of feasting and drunken revelry.

◇ ◇ ◇

While Antony was thus engaged in drunken revelry in Italy, his army was in Syria under the command of Ventidius. There it put the warlike Parthians to flight and won still greater glory for their general's name.

In Rome again, the matter of young upstart Pompey settled, Caesar and Antony prepared to part and passed Octavia from a brother's to a husband's hand to bind their alliance tight.

In Egypt, Queen Cleopatra sent for the hapless messenger who had brought the news of Antony's new marriage. Her first terror at the loss of Antony grown calmer, her curiosity was restless. What was the Roman woman like?

'Is she as tall as me?' she demanded.

'She is not, madam,' replied the messenger, cautiously.

'Did you hear her speak? Is she shrill-tongued or low?'

'She is low-voiced,' the answer came.

'Dull of tongue and dwarfish!' scorned Cleopatra. 'Guess at her years,' she demanded.

'I do think she's thirty,' the messenger warmed to his task, and so the study of her rival's charms progressed, Cleopatra showering the messenger with promised gifts of gold for every pale description given. Antony could not wish to stay with Octavia for long!

◇ ◇ ◇

Antony had gone to Athens with Octavia. But as Enobarbus had foretold, the new-sealed friendship with her distant brother Caesar did not last. Old angers bred anew between the rivals. Publicly Caesar condemned Antony. New wars were brewed against Pompey ...

Octavia, pawn in the game of power between her brother and her husband, struggled with the role of peacemaker, pleading with Antony to put his grievances aside.

He agreed that she could try her pleas for reconciliation, be ambassador between them. Yet in the same breath, he vowed to begin his preparations for a war that would eclipse her brother.

'War between you two would be as if the world should cleave, and that slain men should solder up the rift,' she cried in fear and misery.

Now the rivalries burst from their bonds. Caesar and Lepidus made war on Pompey: no sooner was Pompey dead, than Caesar accused Lepidus of treachery with Pompey and imprisoned the ageing triumvir.

Antony and Caesar were poised, alone, against each other. On their choices hung the course of peace, or the headlong plunge into the bloody chaos of new wars. With Octavia gone to plead for reconciliation with her brother, the last remaining bond with Rome was lost.

Antony went to Cleopatra.

In Rome, with mounting fury, Caesar heard that Antony had abandoned Octavia, condemned Rome publicly, and bequeathed his empire to Cleopatra. Enthroned on chairs of gold in the public marketplace in Alexandria, beside a Cleopatra splendid in the robes of the Goddess Isis, their children grouped around them, Antony had given her Egypt, lower Syria, Cyprus, Lydia: of all these he made her absolute queen. Their sons he had proclaimed the kings of kings, giving them Great Media, Parthia, Armenia, Syria, Cilicia and Phoenicia ...

War loomed closer: Antony accused Caesar of seizing Sicily from Pompey, yet not giving Antony his share; of not returning ships loaned for war; deposing Lepidus and taking his territories and revenues for himself. Caesar sent replies: he would grant Antony part of what he had conquered, but demanded equally his share of Armenia and Antony's other kingdoms in the east, those he was busy giving away to Cleopatra ...

Neither yielded. Antony assembled the kings of the earth for war: King Herod of Jewry, the kings of Libya, Cappadocia, Paphlagonia, Thracia, Arabia, Pont, Comagen, Mede and Lycaonia ...

◊ ◊ ◊

Enobarbus and Antony's other officers watched Cleopatra's involvement in the coming war uneasily.

'It is said in Rome that your maids

manage this war!' Enobarbus told her sharply.

'Sink Rome, and their tongues rot that speak against us!' Cleopatra cried.

Even as they argued, Antony appeared, exclaiming at the lightning movement of Caesar's fleet across the Ionian Sea towards them. 'Canidius,' he told his commanding officer, 'we will fight him by sea.'

'By sea! what else?' nodded Cleopatra.

'Why will my lord do so?' Canidius enquired, perturbed.

'Because he dares us to it,' said Antony, and smiled at Cleopatra.

'Your ships are not well manned,' protested Enobarbus. 'Your sailors are mule drivers, reapers, people swiftly pressed into this war; in Caesar's fleet are those that have often against Pompey fought: their ships are nimble, yours, heavy. No disgrace shall fall on you for refusing him at sea, being prepared for land!'

'By sea, by sea,' repeated Antony, deaf to all argument.

'You therein throw away the absolute soldiership you have by land, distract your army which consists of war-marked footsoldiers. You leave unused your skills—'

'I'll fight at sea,' said Antony impatiently.

'I have sixty sailing ships, Caesar has none better,' Cleopatra said.

They would hear no argument: Canidius must maintain the nineteen legions and twelve-thousand cavalry of Antony's mighty army unused on land until the battle fought by sea was over.

And all the while, with dazzling speed, Caesar's fleet and army neared. On the plains of Macedonia, he gave his final orders to his commanding officer: 'Strike not by land; keep whole: provoke not battle till we have done at sea. Do not exceed the order, for our fortune lies upon this risk!'

◇ ◇ ◇

At Actium off the coast of Macedonia, the rival fleets engaged, while on the land the two great armies held aloof. At the bloody peak of battle, while all around men threw their lives behind Mark Antony, Cleopatra's flagship hoisted sail and fled, her fleet of sixty flying in panic with her.

The thousands on Antony's ships watched in disbelief: their mighty general, bound to the Egyptian queen by invisible bonds of self-destruction, turned and took flight after her.

'We have kissed away kingdoms and provinces!' a soldier cried to Enobarbus. 'She once being turned, the noble ruin of her magic, Antony, claps on his sea-wing and, like a doting duck, flies after her: I never saw an action of such shame!'

It spelled the doom of Antony. Had Antony held steady, their fortunes on the sea might well have triumphed. Now, his forces began to crumble: six kings of Antony's eastern empire yielded at once to Caesar. Canidius, devastated by his general's desertion from the fight, prepared also to leave and join his legions to the victorious Octavius Caesar.

'I'll yet follow the wounded chance of Antony,' Enobarbus said, 'though my reason sits in the wind against me.'

◇ ◇ ◇

Antony plunged into a despair so deep it seemed to him the land itself was ashamed to bear him. He urged his remaining followers to fly, to take his ship and gold and make their peace with Caesar.

'Where have you led me, Egypt?' he turned on Cleopatra bitterly.

'Oh, my lord, my lord,' she moaned, 'forgive my fearful sails! I little thought you would have followed!'

'You knew too well my heart was to your rudder tied by the strings and you would tow me after: and that your call might from the bidding of the gods command me!' he cried.

'Oh, my pardon,' was all the queen could say, for the enormity of what had happened struck her almost dumb.

Antony buried his face in his hands. Wherever he looked he seemed to see the image of Octavius Caesar rise and look down with disdain upon the shattered greatness of Mark Antony. A mighty general who could let judgement that had once commanded half the world, now ride upon his passions into the heart of his own doom. 'Now I must to the young man send humble treaties, dodge and

shuffle in the shifts of lowness,' Antony mourned. 'I, who with half the bulk of the world played as I pleased, making and marring fortunes.'

He reached suddenly for Cleopatra, hopelessness and anger mingled in his love. 'You did know how much you were my conqueror,' he whispered.

'Pardon, pardon,' she wept.

He raised her face to his. 'Fall not a tear,' he told her, gentle, again. 'Give me a kiss. Even this repays me ...'

◇   ◇   ◇

To victorious Caesar, encamped in Egypt, they sent their petitions: for Antony, permission to remain in Egypt or live a private man in Athens. For Cleopatra, rule of Egypt back, for her and all her heirs.

Caesar had no ears for Antony's request. For Cleopatra there was a stark answer, starkly given. She could have her wishes, on condition that she drove Antony from Egypt or killed him there.

'To the boy Caesar send this grizzled head, and he will fill your wishes to the brim,' Antony told her.

'That head, my lord?' faltered Cleopatra, struck dumb by the enormity of the demand.

There was no pause in the conqueror's assault upon her. Hard on the heels of the first, a second ambassador was sent to win her from Antony. Cleopatra, crushed by the vastness of her fall with Antony from queen of a gigantic empire to a beggar even for her life, finally saw the magnitude of their common ruin.

She eyed Caesar's ambassador cautiously, feeling her way in untried territory towards some escape from their predicament. 'Tell Octavius I am prompt to lay my crown at his feet, and there to kneel,' she said. 'Tell him, from his all-obeying breath I hear the doom of Egypt.'

Searching her words for some promise of the betrayal of Antony, the ambassador urged, 'It is your noblest course,' and with the boldness of a messenger sent by the conqueror of the world, he moved forward and pressed his lips upon her hand.

Antony, coming suddenly upon his love in close and familiar conference with his enemy's ambassador, saw it with the burn of jealousy, saw only betrayal. Savagely he had the ambassador dragged away for whipping till he ran with blood.

'You were half-blasted before I knew you,' he raged at Cleopatra, 'a deceiver ever.'

'Is it come to this?' whispered Cleopatra, whose groping towards a path for her survival had nevertheless not yet encompassed the betrayal of her love.

'Alack,' cried Antony, 'our moon is now eclipsed; and it portends alone the fall of Antony!'

But yet, again, before the hour was gone, she drew him to her, and Antony, his rage and jealousy now spent, grasped at her words of love as though they were sap to renew his faltering limbs. He soared suddenly towards new energy. He would rally his remaining forces and throw their fates upon another try at Caesar!

'Do you hear, lady?' he cried, 'If from the field I shall return once more to kiss these lips, I will appear in blood: I and my sword will earn our place in history: there's hope in it yet! Come, let's have another gaudy night: call to me all my sad captains! Let's mock the midnight bell!'

Only Enobarbus, listening, understood the finality of the impending doom. 'Now he'll outstare the lightning!' he said, with miserable disbelief. He shook his head. Now he knew that even he, who had withstood the massing failures of Antony's wild choices, even he, the most faithful of all followers, would leave Antony.

◊ ◊ ◊

Antony rose higher on the crest of defiance; in a kind of ecstasy, he prepared to fight by sea and land to reverse his fortunes.

Caesar prepared by land and sea to complete the final defeat of Antony. He spoke of the nearing time of universal peace across the Roman world.

Enobarbus succumbed to his despair for Antony, and went to Caesar's camp. Yet he loathed what he had done and writhed with the poison of his betrayal.

Antony, strapped in his warrior's armour by Cleopatra's hands, marched with spirits high towards the port where ranks of men armoured for war awaited him. There he learned bitterly that Enobarbus had left him.

The bitterness was not for Enobarbus; it was for himself. In his friend's

betrayal, he understood those truths about himself which he refused to recognize. 'Oh, my fortunes have corrupted honest men!' he cried, and gave swift orders that Enobarbus' treasure be sent after him, along with gentle greetings and farewells.

Enobarbus learned of his deserted general's generosity, and knew he could not fight against him. 'No,' he cried, 'I will go seek some ditch wherein to die!'

◇ ◇ ◇

That day brought unforeseen success for Antony: 'We have beat Caesar to his camp,' he cried exultantly. 'Run on before and let the queen know of our actions! Tomorrow, before the sun shall see us, we'll spill the blood that has today escaped. I thank you all!' he hailed his followers.

In Caesar's camp, by night, the sentinels found the dying Enobarbus, who in his misery fell with the name of Antony upon his lips.

◇ ◇ ◇

The second day of battle dawned. Again, as once before, Antony threw all into the fight by sea. Again, as once before, he lost all. Cleopatra's fleet surrendered to the enemy.

'Betrayed I am,' he cried. 'Oh, this false soul of Egypt! This charm, whose eye called forth my wars, then called them home, has fast and loose beguiled me to the very heart of loss.'

Cleopatra shook before the onrush of his fury and his belief that she'd conspired with Caesar for his doom. In panic she took refuge from him in a monument. And in her desperation to regain his love, sent word that she had killed herself and died with Antony's name escaping from her lips.

In equal haste she despatched her attendant to find out how Antony might take her death, so as to know how she might plot her onward course.

'I made these wars for Egypt,' moaned Antony, 'and the queen, whose heart I thought I had, for she had mine, she has packed cards with Caesar and false played my glory for an enemy's triumph.'

Into the mire of his despair came the false news of Cleopatra's death, richly embroidered by the lavish tongue of her attendant – how she had gasped her last with Antony's name upon her lips.

'Dead, then?' he said, and trembled at it. A moment before he had raged for her death, but now he knew that the long day's task for him was over. No more to do but to unarm, to throw off the warrior's clothes in which, so many years ago he'd come to her, and in which, on this dark day, he had lost her.

'I will overtake you, Cleopatra,' he breathed to the glorious queen who'd bound his heart and mind and soul even to this orgy of destruction. 'I will overtake you, and weep for my pardon. I come, my queen, stay for me; where souls do couch on flowers, we'll go hand in hand, and with our sprightly port make the ghosts gaze ...'

Desperately, he begged his last and faithful follower, his page, to end the life of fallen Antony. The page, refusing to the last to look upon the ruin of his master, killed himself instead.

Antony was alone. He yearned to escape the abyss of loneliness and dishonour that bared its jaws to swallow him. There was no one to help. In this final hour, only himself. He threw himself forward on his sword. But, in grotesque mockery of this day's failure, he did not die.

He called the guards. They backed in horror from his writhing form, and would not give the final stroke.

'Most absolute lord,' a voice came through his agony, 'my mistress sent me to you.' And then he knew. Cleopatra's final, fatal game with him to buy her life, had bought his death. In a sudden premonition that he would kill himself, she had sent her servant to reveal the truth to him, too late.

'Bear me, good friends,' he begged his guards, 'to where Cleopatra waits. It is the last service that I shall command you.'

◇ ◇ ◇

Barricaded high up in the monument, Cleopatra saw the dying form of Antony, and all the ebb and flow of her passionate struggle to survive swelled like a darkness that would smother her.

'Oh sun, burn the great sphere you move in!' she cried. 'Darkling stand the varying shore of the world! Oh Antony, Antony, Antony! Help, Charmian, help, Iras,' she begged her attendants, 'help, friends below, let's draw him up.'

'I am dying, Egypt, dying,' came Antony's hoarse whisper, as his bleeding body was hoisted to them in the monument. 'Oh quick, or I am gone.'

'Oh welcome, welcome!' she cried. She clasped his head and smothered it with kisses. 'Die, where you have lived: quicken with kissing!' She clung to him. 'Will you die?' she sobbed, feeling his life ebbing. 'Shall I abide in this dull world, which in your absence is no better than a sty?'

He struggled to persuade her: make peace with Caesar, save herself! But as the last breath faded from Mark Antony, the Queen of Egypt seemed to tremble. His life, flying, took with it the flame of hers and left only the embers. Her cry rose in a shrill wail of devastation above the darkness of the monument.

'Oh see, my women, the crown of the earth melts, and there is nothing left remarkable beneath the visiting moon!'

◇ ◇ ◇

News of Antony's death reached Caesar fast, even with the sword with which he'd killed himself, as proof ...

Caesar stared at the pitiful thing in silence. 'The breaking of so great a thing should make a greater crack,' he said at last. 'The death of Antony is not a single doom; in the name lay half the world.'

And now he thought of Cleopatra, whose presence as the vanquished Queen

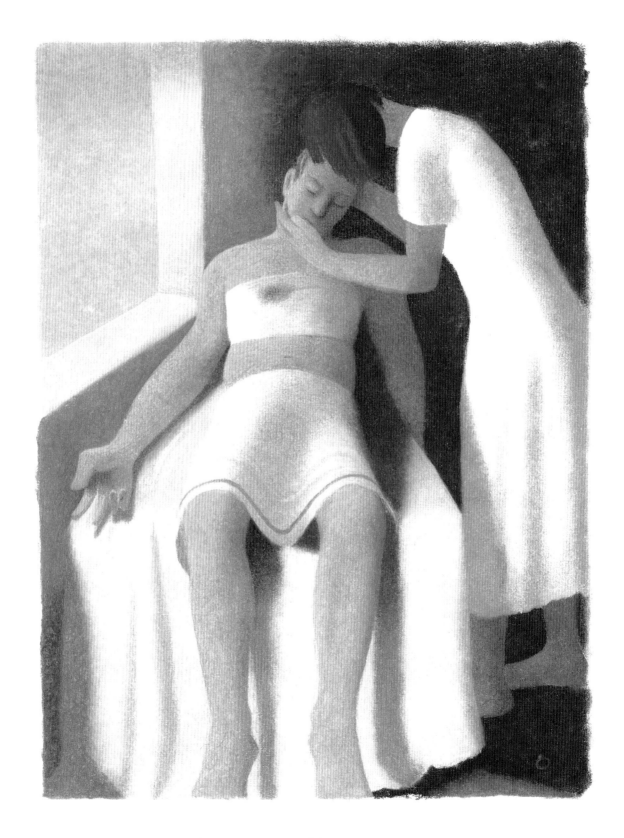

of Egypt in Rome would make absolute his triumph from this conquest. He gave orders that she should be captured from the monument and watched with care. She must commit no act of suicide which would defeat his final victory.

Cleopatra, knowing that he planned to show her in his triumph in Rome, receded into memories of glorious Antony, and waited only for her moment of escape.

◊   ◊   ◊

Caesar came to see the queen whose love had fired his rival to the brink of self-destruction. She kneeled low before the Emperor of the Roman world. She acknowledged his absolute mastery over all the territory that had once been hers to rule. She called out her treasurer to give evidence of her possessions, all, she claimed, nothing withheld from Caesar's eye.

Not so, the treasurer denied. She had withheld enough to purchase what she wanted.

She flinched before her treasurer's desertion to her will. It was the ultimate treachery, the blow that signalled the finality of her doom before the triumph of Octavius Caesar. Not even this much loyalty could she command, once fallen from her power. Now she heard Caesar's promise that he meant no harm to her, and nodded her acceptance of his absolute mastery.

Caesar left her.

'Now, Charmian,' Cleopatra whispered. 'Show me, my women, like a queen: go fetch my best robes,' and dreamy with the memory, she murmured, 'I am again for Cydnus, to meet Mark Antony! Bring my crown and all ...'

They prepared. Unsuspecting, the guard let in an old man carrying a basket, so he said, of figs. The basket placed before the dreaming queen, the old man left.

'Give me my robe, put on my crown,' Cleopatra spoke. 'I have immortal longings in me. Quickly, quickly, good Iras,' she urged her young attendant. 'I think I hear Antony call. I see him rouse himself to praise my noble act. I hear him mock the luck of Caesar. Husband,' she cried to Antony, 'I come!'

She reached into the basket at her feet. She lifted from beneath the leaves a writhing snake, a poisonous asp of the life-giving River Nile.

'Come,' she spoke caressingly to it, 'with your sharp teeth this knot of life at once untie.' She placed the creature to her breast. She closed her eyes. She seemed to wander in a dream again. 'Peace, peace,' she chided Charmian, whose sobs

broke through her vision of death. 'Peace! Do you not see my baby at my breast, that sucks the nurse asleep? As sweet as balm, as soft as air, as gentle,' she crooned to the instrument of her escape into the world where Antony awaited her.

And so they found her, glorious in her death as she had been in life when she had captured Antony upon the golden barge at Cydnus. At peace she sat, as though no more than slumbering. At her feet lay Iras, choosing death beside her royal mistress, and Charmian, who in a loving trance arranged the royal crown with gentle care before she too crumbled to the ground and died.

Around their bodies only the glistening trail of the poisonous asp bore witness to their choice.

Caesar knew then that Egypt's queen, in this her final act, defeated him.

'Take up her bed, and bear her women from the monument,' he said, quietly. 'She shall be buried by her Antony: no grave upon the earth shall clip in it a pair so famous.'

And even Octavius Caesar, emperor of the whole world, paused for that moment in his relentless march to power to bow his head before the pity of their story, as great as was the once-remembered glory of Mark Antony.

◇ ◇ ◇

OTHELLO

THE TWO MEN MOVED BETWEEN THE ARCHES, soft-footed in the shadows of the walls. Iago, in front, talked in quick, sharp tones; behind him scuffled Roderigo, straining to hear his every word. They had one purpose, and their goal was near at hand. Steadily they moved across the dark expanses of the square between the sleeping houses; Iago slid into the shadow of an arch and motioned Roderigo on, into the entrance to Brabantio's house. Roderigo obeyed Iago's nod. He turned his face up to the window.

'What, ho, Brabantio! Signior Brabantio! Ho!' he yelled.

Shrouded in the darkness, Iago raised his cry. 'Awake! Brabantio! Thieves! Look to your house, your daughter and your bags! Thieves!'

Brabantio's face thrust from the window high above their heads.

'Signior!' yelled Roderigo, warming to the task. 'Is all your family within?'

The old man peered into the ill-lit square. Who were these two? The one he recognized, that idiot Roderigo who haunted his door, mooning for his daughter, Desdemona. The other he could not see …

'Are your doors locked?' Iago cried. 'Sir, you've been robbed. Your heart is burst, you have lost your soul! Your daughter and the Moor …'

Fear pierced the sleep-sodden face of the old man. 'Give me a light!' he roared. 'Light, I say, light!' And as the cry was raised in panic through his house, amid the flare of torches and the sounds of running feet, Iago melted into the shadows. He could rely on Roderigo now to play upon this father's terrors for his fair white daughter, stolen off into the lover's arms of black Othello, the Moor.

Iago had other, urgent tasks, that could not be done if he were seen here, where the seeds were being sown against the Moor. He must fly back to stand beside Othello, to show the flag and sing of love, for was he not the trusted ensign of this noble Moor? Was he not honest Iago, outspoken, true and indispensable at his great master's side?

Othello was a man of some considerable repute in Venice: of royal Moorish blood, a soldier, famed for military success, known for his nobility, wisdom, experience and skills. No other general could lead the Venetian forces in the wars in Cyprus against the Turks.

Why then did Iago plant these seeds of venom against the Moor? Did even Iago know? Always he had hated Othello. Contempt for this most powerful black man was woven round Iago like a skin: he moved always within it. One grudge could no longer be separated from another; he could not say which fed the next, or which was the spring from which the others flowed. True, Othello had not made Iago his lieutenant, his second-in-command – a post for which he was well qualified by skill, experience and long-standing service beside the Moor. Othello had instead preferred another, one Michael Cassio, and Iago remained his ensign, the lowest rank of officer.

Yet this grievance only served to fire already smouldering flames. He hated the honoured Moor, gigantic in his power and reputation. He hated: and he longed for vengeance. But no small punishment would be enough: it must be grand, colossal, monstrous in its finality ...

Othello was at the height of power: adorned in glory, decked with riches by the Venetian state for services in war. Each senator felt keenly how the health of the state hung on Othello's skills and reputation in these dangerous times of war. Today Othello had secretly married the daughter of the senator, Signior Brabantio, that same senator that Iago and Roderigo had so rudely wakened from his sleep. But Iago was ready to poison the Moor's delight, and to begin tonight. With swift foot and still swifter tongue he reached Othello to tell of Brabantio's imminent attack on him.

Othello listened with half an ear. Everything was coloured by his love for Desdemona, and he knew that his services to Venice spoke far louder than anyone's anger about this marriage.

He waited calmly for her father. Others reached him first: his lieutenant, Michael Cassio, and officers of the Duke of Venice, requesting his immediate attendance at a full session of the Senate concerning the wars in Cyprus.

But now there was a rumbling murmur in the streets and the ominous flare of torches carried by many men: Brabantio and his friends approached with weapons drawn, led on by Roderigo.

'Down with him, thief!' Brabantio was shouting.

Cassio and his companions instantly drew swords to defend Othello.

Othello did not stir. He raised a hand above the uproar.

'Put away your bright swords, for the dew will rust them,' he said, and his deep, unhurried tones dropped across the tumult like a rich cloak to douse rebellious flames.

'Foul thief! Where have you stowed my daughter?' Brabantio shouted, incensed by this further proof of Othello's devilish powers. Already the Moor had used them on his daughter, for what other cause than such black witchcraft could make her shun the suitors of her own kind and fly to the bosom of such a man as this?

'Damned as you are,' he shouted, 'you have enchanted her! You have abused her delicate youth with drugs or minerals. Take hold of him! If he resists, subdue him at his peril!'

The Moor stood quietly. He made no move as swords were raised against him, except that single motion of the hand which compelled the weapons down again.

'Where do you want me to go to answer this your charge?' he enquired softly of Brabantio.

'To prison,' the old senator spat his reply.

But now the Duke's officers intervened impatiently. The Duke's summons was being ignored. They were all wanted at the Senate, now: Othello, and the senator, Signior Brabantio.

Brabantio was suddenly satisfied. The Senate, in full session in the dead of night, could hear his cause!

Iago followed Othello out. His face spoke volumes of anxious worry at this attack upon the honour of his master. But his inner thoughts were of a very different colour ...

◊　◊　◊

The Senate was in uproar. A Turkish fleet was moving to attack the Venetian colony at Cyprus and instant help needed for the island's garrison. Only the General Othello could be sent for such a weighty task.

But Brabantio's grief intruded: he forced his fellow senators to hear: his daughter had been abused, stolen from him, corrupted!

By whom? In consternation the senators saw his finger pointed at the Moor on whom their hope of fortune in the wars now rested!

The Moor nodded. He had married Brabantio's daughter. 'Send for the lady,' he said. 'Let her speak of me before her father.' And while the senators waited for her, he spoke to them of how the gentle daughter of Brabantio had learned to love him; and as he told them, his face was captured by the wonder of the memories.

'Her father often invited me,' he said, with a slow look at fuming Brabantio. 'He would ask me the story of my life from year to year, the battles, sieges, fortunes that I have known. I spoke of being taken and sold into slavery, of vast caves and idle deserts, rough quarries, rocks and hills, whose heads touch heaven ...'

And so the Moor spoke on, the rich tapestry of his enormous life moving across his face. Closer the tale had drawn Brabantio's daughter, Desdemona; she had given him a world of sighs for the pains that he had suffered. 'She loved me for the dangers I had passed, and I loved her that she did pity them. This,' he turned now to the senators, 'this is the only witchcraft I have used.'

'I think this tale would win my daughter too,' the Duke of Venice murmured, with a smile.

And Desdemona, entering with her exquisite face aglow as was the Moor's, had eyes only for Othello. Though she addressed her father in loving tones, her words told only of her final, absolute loyalty to this, her chosen husband, lord and love, the Moor.

Iago knew then his scheme had foundered on the rocks of Desdemona's love and Othello's faith in her. His hatred burned a little higher. There was no simple trap to catch this man. It needed a web of infinite proportions, woven with the utmost skill.

'Look to her, Moor,' he heard the thwarted father mutter. 'Look to her, if you have eyes to see; she has deceived her father, and may deceive you.'

'I stake my life upon her faithfulness,' Othello dismissed the father's words, and turned to his wife with a loving gaze.

In the silence of the Senate court after they had gone, Roderigo sulked. Iago's scheme to separate Desdemona from the Moor might have opened the field to him again. 'I will drown myself,' he muttered piteously.

'Come, be a man! Drown yourself? Drown cats and blind puppies!' Iago put his arm about Roderigo's shoulders. This first stab had not pierced its target as he hoped, but still he needed Roderigo as an ally. 'Put money in your purse,' he urged. 'Follow these wars. Desdemona must get bored with the Moor!' and if Roderigo were near at hand, well ...! Hope flickered across Roderigo's disappointed face. 'No more of drowning, do you hear?' Iago urged.

His mood restored, Roderigo enthusiastically assured his friend. 'I'll go sell all my land!'

Alone, Iago could feel the threads of a design that gathered in his mind, a web that would ensnare them both, Othello and the favoured Cassio. He searched his mind, and searched again. Desdemona! At the centre of his design, Desdemona would be the bait.

But the threads still floated, unconnected, their ends free ... then in a moment he had caught and knitted them. Michael Cassio! He would make Othello think his beloved, faithful wife was locked in some faithlessness with Cassio.

◇ ◇ ◇

Othello gave his new wife to Iago's care and, before the break of dawn, set sail with Cassio for Cyprus. Iago, with his own wife, Emilia, and Desdemona, followed in another ship. But raging storms wrecked the Turkish fleet and ended all threat of their attack. The Venetian ships, though driven wide apart, survived and finally reached Cyprus.

So they gathered on the island, like flies drawn in to Iago's spinning web. Cassio's ship came first. Then Iago's with Emilia and Desdemona. And finally Othello, hailed by a jubilant population as the hero who would deliver them from all menace of the Turks.

Othello had eyes for no one but Desdemona. There could be no wonder greater than this overwhelming joy at seeing her, and she him, longing to be in each other's arms and close the world away.

Iago watched. How well-tuned they were for him to play on! And so too was Roderigo, lingering like a love-lorn puppy to glimpse Desdemona.

First, he must tune up Roderigo. With swift strokes it was done. Did Roderigo see this Cassio? Not only had he usurped Iago's place as Othello's second-in-command, but also he claimed Desdemona's love! She loved Cassio now, bored as she was with the coarse qualities of the Moor! So (he explained carefully – Roderigo's brain could hold so little at a time) now Cassio had her; until he was removed, there was no hope for Roderigo.

'Watch tonight,' Iago encouraged him. 'Find some occasion to anger Cassio. He is rash and very sudden in his anger, and may strike you.'

And so was the first thread spun: envious Roderigo to deal with Michael Cassio. Now to the Moor. Iago must put the Moor into a jealousy so strong that judgement could not cure it. He would use Cassio to bring down a double enemy.

◊ ◊ ◊

There was much feasting and jollity that night in Cyprus: a double celebration – the Turkish fleet destroyed and great Othello's wedding. Having sailed from Venice

on the same night that he had married, Othello's first union with Desdemona would be here on Cyprus.

Othello left the garrison in Cassio's capable hands, and Cassio would command the island's guard with Ensign Iago's help.

And what a jovial fellow this Iago was, Cassio soon discovered: quick with a jest, a song, full of good humour and generous with wine to drink Othello's health (though Cassio resisted strongly, for he had no head for drinking). Others came to join them: merry souls, among them Signior Montano, governor of Cyprus, who had sent for Othello's help. He too brought wine ...

It was not long before good Cassio's words grew slurred. He staggered a little, though he protested loudly that he was not drunk. He stumbled away, earnestly assuring them that he could do his duty as well as any sober man.

As Cassio left, Iago's face became a mask of sorrow. What a vice this drunkenness was, he murmured to Montano. Cassio – so fine a soldier, so trusted by Othello – yet every night he was like this ...

Roderigo, of course, was skulking in the shadows. Secret signals from Iago sent him to follow Cassio. Just as Iago planned, drunken Cassio now blundered through their midst in hot pursuit of Roderigo, throwing wild blows and kicks and waving a sword furiously.

Montano instantly leapt to catch and calm him; Cassio was so inflamed with drink that he yelled and staggered, swung his sword wildly at the governor and pierced his arm.

All the while Iago drew Roderigo off, seeming to give chase. 'Away!' he hissed. 'Go out and cry mutiny!' The hideous clamour of a bell rang out and panic spread like fire through the town.

'Hold!' Othello's tones boomed like a cannon across the uproar. Stung from his wedding bed by the clamour, Othello surveyed them all in disbelief. What barbarous brawl was this? What dreadful bell clanging to

turn the island's people to blind terror! He rounded on his ensign. 'Honest Iago, speak. Who began this?'

Iago would say nothing, though his face was creased with grief.

Cassio, swaying in drunken stupor, could say nothing.

'Worthy Othello,' Montano gasped in pain. 'I am hurt. Your officer, Iago, can inform you.'

Othello grew angry. His officers and his guard brawling, with weapons drawn!

'Inform me,' he said, in a low and menacing voice, 'how this foul rout began. What! In a town of war, the people's hearts brimful of fear, to follow private and domestic quarrels in the night! It is monstrous! Iago, who began it?'

'If you tell more or less than the truth you are no soldier,' Montano panted to Iago, nearly fainting with his wound.

A pain seemed to shadow Iago's face. 'I had rather have this tongue cut from my mouth than it should harm Michael Cassio,' he said. Haltingly, as if each word were a new hurt upon a loyal friend, he let out the tale: Cassio had pursued some stranger, Montano stepped in to calm him, he himself had given chase, the stranger had outrun him. 'Yet surely,' he added, 'Cassio must have received from him that fled some terrible insult.'

Othello looked long and hard at Iago. How clearly he could see that Iago's honesty and love tried to put less blame on Cassio!

Cassio steeled his spinning brain to receive the general's wrath. But there were only quiet, damning words: 'Cassio, I love you well. But never more be an officer of mine.' Othello turned and left.

Cassio sank to his knees. The full meaning of what Othello said now pierced the haze clouding his sodden brain. 'Reputation, reputation, reputation! I have lost my reputation! Iago!'

Iago rushed to him with swift concern. All was not lost. Cassio must approach the general, make amends, and get his position back. Why not try to win the help of Desdemona, for there could be no voice more powerful to move the Moor. 'Beg her help to put you in your place again. She is so free, so kind. Entreat her to bind up this broken joint between you and her husband,' Iago urged.

A ray of hope lit up the eyes of Cassio; and Iago saw the thread of his own marvellous web spin on. While Cassio begged Desdemona to repair his fortunes, and she pleaded for him with the Moor, so would Iago pour into Othello's ear the poison that her pleas flowed only from a lust for Cassio. And so would Iago, out of Desdemona's goodness, make the net to enmesh them all ...

◇   ◇   ◇

In the garden of the castle the following morning, Cassio spoke to Desdemona. He heard from her own lips that she would give Othello no rest until Cassio was restored to favour; she knew well his loyalty and long-standing, trusted friendship with the Moor.

But seeing Othello himself approaching, ashamed to face him, Cassio hastily took leave of Desdemona and disappeared.

Iago was leading Othello to where he knew this meeting was taking place. He paused, as though surprised to see Cassio there. He let a mutter slither from his lips, 'Ha! I like not that!' Just loud enough.

'What do you say?' Othello asked. He waved affectionately to Desdemona. 'Was that not Cassio parted from my wife?'

'Cassio, my lord?' Iago's voice spoke volumes of surprise. 'I cannot think why he would steal away so guiltily seeing you coming!'

'I do believe it was he,' Othello assured him, puzzled.

But the puzzlement was in a moment gone. He stretched his arms, and lifted up his face to feel the balmy air: such contentment since he had stepped on to this island! Here he had reached the zenith of his love for Desdemona; no pinnacle could reach higher, no peak could be more perfect than his adoration for this woman who had, against all opposition, chosen him.

She had seen him arrive. True to her promise to Lieutenant Cassio, she took up his cause. 'Good, my lord, if I have any grace or power to move you, I beg you, call Cassio back.'

'Not now, sweet Desdemona, some other time,' Othello told her gently, smiling a little at her earnestness.

'But shall it be shortly?' she persisted.

'The sooner, sweet, for you,' he assured her.

'Shall it be tonight, at supper?' she pressed him.

'No, not tonight.'

'Tomorrow then, or Tuesday morn, or Tuesday noon or night. I beg you, name the time, but let it not be longer than three days.'

Watching her face so fired with her sincerity, Othello felt that he would swoon. Her look, the perfume of her skin, her nearness, overwhelmed him. So much he loved her now! 'I will deny you nothing,' he murmured, and took her in his arms; and she, content with this, withdrew.

'How I do love you,' he whispered after her. 'And when I do not love you, chaos is come again!'

'My noble lord,' Iago broke in upon his thoughts.

'What do you say, Iago?' Othello asked, jovially.

'Did Michael Cassio, when you wooed my lady, know of your love?'

'He did, from first to last: why do you ask?'

Iago seemed to ponder. 'I did not think he had been acquainted with her,' he replied, as though this thought were the slightest morsel in the world.

'Oh yes, and went between us very often,' Othello said.

'Indeed!'

'Indeed!' Othello mimicked him, 'Aye, indeed,' he snorted. What did Iago think that meant? 'Is he not honest?' he teased, knowing the answer without any doubt.

'Honest, my lord!' said Iago, slowly, considering the word.

And so he began: a look, a pause, a question, a smothered exclamation, a sideways slither of his eyes. So did Iago weave, with thread on thread, his web: a pattern, gossamer light at first, of fancies that touched Othello, quick, at once dismissed, and then returned, for Iago to tease them out ...

Was Cassio honest? Iago thought he was, and men should be what they seem to be ...

'By heaven, I'll know your thoughts,' Othello cried, for now a worm had entered him, a small gnawing worm. Though he knew there was no reason to doubt Desdemona's honesty, though he knew she loved him passionately and had endured her father's wrath to follow him, yet now, slowly, the worm began to eat its way into his certainties.

'Oh beware, my lord, of jealousy!' Iago burst out, as if prompted by a passion stronger than he could master. 'It is the green-eyed monster which mocks the meat it feeds on!'

'Oh misery!' Othello's knowledge of his wife warred with terrors he had never felt before. Though a part of him knew that he must, he could no longer turn away from the vile pattern that Iago spun. He knew his wife was honest and that Cassio was honest. Yet he knew also that Iago was honest and would not hint at such things to tear his soul without good cause!

Then he remembered once again the strength of Desdemona's love, and he felt a surge of faith in her. 'I will not doubt her,' he told Iago, 'for she had eyes, and she chose me,' and now Othello drew an infinity of strength from this one memory. 'No, Iago,' he declared. 'I'll see before I doubt ...'

'Look to your wife,' was all Iago said. 'Observe her well with Cassio.' The Moor, he pointed out, being a foreigner to Venetian ways, could not expect to know how well-versed the women of Venice were in duping their husbands.

The worm returned, and with it a rotten core of fear eaten by a thousand differences which the Moor felt keenly between himself and all of Venice. He was not one of them. And while his reputation and his power had soared across the gap, now the gap yawned at him with menacing jaws. How well Iago knew how to touch this tender spot so lightly, yet so painfully.

'I think that Desdemona is honest,' Othello said; but on his face had come a haunted look.

But, Iago said, Desdemona turning away from marriage with men of her own kind, might now repent and look again to Venetian men for love ...

A great weariness flowed over Othello now, as though he had lost a battle, and it left him drained on the field. Why had he married? This honest creature, Iago, doubtless saw and knew much more than he unfolded.

'I am abused,' he said the words he feared to say, half question, half statement; and as he said them they took life and became for a moment, true. He gestured Iago away, to leave him to himself. 'My relief must be to loathe her,' he whispered, fearful of the thought.

He heard Desdemona's slight step approach and there was a rush of blood into his head. 'Oh, if she be false, then heaven mocks itself. I'll not believe it!'

Desdemona saw him press his forehead with some pain, and rushed to him. 'Are you not well?'

'I have a pain upon my forehead, here,' he muttered, and turned his gaze from her in misery.

'Let me bind it, hard,' she murmured, softly so as not to hurt his head, and wound her handkerchief about his temples.

'It is too little,' Othello brushed it away. And neither saw the handkerchief fall

to the ground, nor Iago's wife, Emilia, snatch it up.

It was the Moor's first gift to Desdemona, a delicate tracery of strawberries upon a glorious weave of colour. For some reason which Emilia did not know, Iago had asked her to steal it a hundred times. Now she had it, and would take it to him swiftly, to please him.

◊ ◊ ◊

Othello writhed now upon a wrack, enslaved by images that ripped his dreams and tore his brain, so that he could never sleep or stop the thoughts: Desdemona false! His exquisite wife in whom he had vested all the stored-up love of his tempestuous life, toying, laughing, behind his back, with his friend, Cassio!

'Villain!' he seized Iago. 'Give me proof! If you but slander her and torture me— I think my wife is honest, and I think that she is not. I think that you are just, and think that you are not— I'll have some proof!' he shrieked.

Iago had it. He had heard Cassio talking in his sleep of Desdemona, and urging her to take great care to hide their love from the Moor. And was there not a handkerchief of Desdemona's, a wisp of cloth spotted with strawberries?

Othello froze. He hung upon a precipice and looked down into a void ... Iago had seen Cassio wipe his beard with it!

Othello plunged. All certainties collapsed and all was chaos. The noble general who had stood his ground against a thousand foes and stilled the vile outpourings of Brabantio with a hand, now fell before a tempest of fear and bitterness that swallowed him.

'Within these three days,' he muttered viciously, 'let me hear you say, Iago, that Cassio's not alive.'

'My friend is dead; it is done at your request,' Iago promised. And then his master-stroke: 'But let her live ...'

'Damn her!' Othello's savage cry heralded the closing of Iago's web. 'Damn her!'

◊ ◊ ◊

Desdemona fretted at the loss of her much-treasured handkerchief. She kept it always by her, and its disappearance filled her with a nervousness she did not understand. She did not want Othello to find out, for she sensed a gathering cloud about them, and it chilled her. Othello behaved so oddly! He no longer met her eyes, and she could find no cause for it.

She pressed on with her pleas for Cassio, though, for she had promised the good lieutenant that she would; and this, at least, was something she could accomplish in these strange vacant days since Othello had withdrawn from her.

But Othello had a single answer when she spoke of Michael Cassio. He asked her for the handkerchief. He said he had a cold.

She saw at once he knew she did not have it.

'Is it lost? Speak!' he cried, and his voice was thunder in her ears.

'It is not lost!' she grew confused. 'But what if it were?'

'Fetch it,' he stormed. 'Let me see it.'

Desdemona flinched. 'Why so I can, sir. But I will not now. This is a trick to turn me from my pleas for Cassio! Pray you, let Cassio be received again. Talk to me of Cassio,' she said again, as though her fate had locked itself to this one name and she could not let go.

'Away!' bellowed Othello, and thrust her from him. Damned by her own tongue! And he rushed away from his bewildered wife who shrank in terror from this creature of spitting fury. This was not the man that she had married! Transformed beyond all understanding.

◇ ◇ ◇

So fast the blows fell on Othello's mind that he trembled, shrieked, fell into a foaming trance.

'Work on my medicine, work!' Iago breathed. Quickly he told Othello that he'd hear Cassio damned from his own mouth.

Cassio had found a handkerchief in his room and given it to a woman named Bianca who trailed him about the island. He'd asked her to copy the cloth's design of strawberries. Now, beyond Othello's hearing, Iago asked Cassio about Bianca, for he knew that Cassio always laughed at how the woman adored and hunted him, and told merry tales about her.

Othello, hiding, heard Cassio talking of a woman's love and thought he spoke of Desdomona. He saw Bianca throw a wisp of strawberry-spotted cloth at Cassio, angry at a love-token from another woman. Othello's gaze now rested on the handkerchief, on his love for Desdomona, left to flutter on the ground.

'Aye, let her rot,' the rage swelled in his head. 'Let her be damned tonight; for she shall not live! Give me some poison, Iago; this night; this night, Iago!'

'Do it not with poison,' Iago told him softly. 'Strangle her in bed!'

◇ ◇ ◇

Lodovico, a kinsman of Desdemona's, came from Venice bringing messages for Othello. The Moor, he saw, met him with a distracted air; and Desdemona's face was pale, her eyes flicking nervously towards Othello. She spoke of some division between Cassio and her husband which she hoped to heal. Othello seemed to read the letters from the Duke with only half an eye, and was more given to casting vicious glances at his wife and hissing at every mention of Cassio.

The letters commanded Othello to return to Venice and leave the government of Cyprus to Cassio. To the Venetian Senate, Othello's mission here in Cyprus was now done, and they needed him for other duties.

To Othello, this recall from Cyprus seemed further evidence of the deceit by Cassio and his wife.

'Devil!' he shrieked, and struck her full across the face, the red weal of his hand gleaming like a streak of blood across her cheek.

'My lord,' gasped Lodovico, 'this would not be believed in Venice!'

'Devil! Devil! Out of my sight!' was all the answer Othello gave, his face contorted with disgust.

'I will not stay to offend you,' Desdemona whispered through hopeless tears, and backed away. Othello, muttering insults, pursued her off. Lodovico watched the scene with disbelief. Was this the noble Moor believed by Venice's Senate to be sufficient in all things? Was this the nature that passion could not shake?

'He is much changed,' Iago acknowledged regretfully.

'Are his wits safe? Is he not light of brain? To strike his wife!' Lodovico wondered.

'If only,' Iago murmured softly to him, 'if only I knew that stroke would prove the worst!'

◊ ◊ ◊

Othello sent for Desdemona.

'What are you?' he demanded.

'Your wife, my lord,' she said. 'Your true and loyal wife.'

'Come, swear it. Damn yourself,' he hissed. 'Be double-damned, swear you are honest, for heaven truly knows you are as false as hell!'

'To whom, my lord? With whom? How am I false?' she begged. Hopelessness deadened her. She had no further answer for her transformed lord. She seemed to Emilia to be almost asleep.

She asked Emilia to lay her wedding sheets upon the bed that night.

◇ ◇ ◇

Roderigo was impatient with affairs in Cyprus. He had given Iago a wealth of gold and jewels for Desdemona, but she had never sent for him! He began to wonder if he had been deceived.

But, Iago urged, if Roderigo would show his strength of purpose this night – the very next he would have Desdemona! Did Roderigo know that Cassio had been given command in Cyprus, that Othello and Desdemona were going to Mauritania? If Cassio were removed, Othello would have to stay in Cyprus. Only this could prevent the disappearance of Roderigo's love beyond his grasp. Cassio must be killed! Swiftly Iago sketched the scheme ...

◇ ◇ ◇

Desdemona waited for Othello. He had commanded her to dismiss Emilia and go to bed and she was anxious not to offend him further.

A shiver fluttered through her, an ache for the lost warmth of adoration, so richly won, so quickly gone from her beloved husband. Would it return again? She was afraid, and the fear was great, though she could find no words for it. Her eyes fell on the bridal sheets Emilia had laid on the bed.

'If I do die,' she whispered, involuntarily, 'shroud me in one of those same sheets.'

'Come, come,' Emilia chided her. And yet the coldness had touched her heart too and she jumped at shadows ...

◇ ◇ ◇

A dark street near the harbour; whispers; a shape that melted away and left another huddled against the wall. It was Roderigo, fully primed by Iago, waiting by Bianca's door for Cassio to leave. Iago watched. It mattered not at all to him who killed who, for he wanted both to die. Roderigo bleated for his missing jewels, and would soon begin to talk to others ...

It was quickly done. Cassio's confident step; a stab from Roderigo's dagger, and from the hidden Iago a cut into Cassio's leg.

Lodovico, walking with others to his ship, heard loud groans. He searched, and saw Iago running to the scene holding a light. Together they discovered wounded Cassio on the ground, alive, but white with loss of blood, and there Roderigo, stabbed by Cassio. Under cover of the dark, Iago thrust his dagger hard into Roderigo, who in the moment of his death saw the true colours of his friend for the first and only time. But Roderigo's mouth was stopped, and Iago, riding high on such success, knew that on this night his grand design would reach its peak.

◇ ◇ ◇

Desdemona lay between the bridal sheets. It seemed as if she waited, even in her sleep.

Othello moved towards her. He walked in a dream. All rage was stilled, all anger cold. A single purpose moved him on, and in a trance he glided to it, murmuring, thoughts and fears and horrors circling ever in his head.

'Yet I'll not shed her blood,' he whispered, 'nor scar that skin of hers, whiter than snow. Yet she must die, else she'll betray more men.' The thought no longer held its fire for him, as though his memory spoke of a task once given him, not yet accomplished.

He looked up at the lamp. 'Put out the light.' He looked down at her soft face upon the pillow. 'And then put out the light.' But once the light of Desdemona was put out, it could not be rekindled.

He bowed across her, and felt her breath caress his face, a warm, balmy breath that almost caught him in the wonder of his love again. She stirred, and woke, and saw Othello leaning over her, his eyes a deadening mask of darkness.

'Have you prayed tonight, Desdemona? I would not kill your unprepared spirit.'

'Talk you of killing?' she gasped.

'Aye, I do.'

She shrank within the bed. His lowering face, his grim monotony of tone, froze her. Like a child that fears in innocence and does not understand escape, she cringed before the final stroke. And then, as though he could not leave the thought alone, he cried, 'That handkerchief, which I so loved and gave you, you gave to Cassio!'

'No, by my life and soul! Send for the man and ask him!'

'Sweet soul,' he intoned now without emotion. 'Take heed, take heed of lying. You are on your deathbed.'

'I never did offend you in my life. I never gave Cassio tokens of love!'

'He has confessed.'

'He will not say so!'

'No.' The word was final. 'His mouth is stopped.'

Desdemona sank into the pillows. 'He is betrayed, and I undone,' she said. And with these little words she signed the final testimony of guilt for her avenging husband. All pleas of innocence abandoned, she begged desperately for life.

'It is too late,' he said.

He lifted the pillow from the bed, and pressed it on her face, and held it there until all breath of life was stilled.

He kneeled above the deed. In pure whiteness, shrouded in the bridal sheets, his wife lay dead before him. Emilia's knocks broke in upon him. He got up and started for the door, forgot, turned back, stood near the bed, remembered the knock again, remembered the bed, and drew the curtains round it. He went now to the door.

As Emilia rushed in, there was a gasp of fleeting life from Desdemona. 'Falsely, falsely murdered!'

Emilia wrenched the curtains back and tried to rouse her.

'A guiltless death I die,' the words fell from her paling lips.

'Who has done this?' Emilia wept.

'Nobody, I myself. Farewell,' and Desdemona died.

'She's like a liar gone to burning hell,' Othello screamed. 'It was I that killed her!'

'The more angel she, and you the blacker devil!' Emilia rounded on him. In disbelief she heard him spit his accusations: Desdemona false, Desdemona locked in lust with Cassio! 'Your husband knew it all!'

Emilia stopped. She heard the words again. Husband. She repeated it. Once, twice, a third time. Suddenly she saw the web her husband spun, and understood.

She shrieked for help. They came rushing to her cries, and broke in upon the dreadful scene: Montano, Lodovico, others; and Iago, hot to see his handiwork.

But he had left one thread of his design imperfect. He had not seen how Emilia loved Desdemona. Now this love would not be stilled for anyone! Desdemona false, Emilia shouted. A vicious lie!

A light began to dawn in Othello's mangled mind. But yet it had to fight the darkness of Iago's poison. 'The handkerchief,' he whispered. 'The handkerchief.'

Then Emilia truly understood. And as she turned, her face aflame with knowledge of her husband's evil, Iago saw his end in sight. He rushed at her and drove his dagger hard into her heart, and fled.

Now Othello knew, as well. He felt the web of lies which spun its tissues round and through his mind, silencing his judgement, and killing his humanity. He had become that savage thing that Iago always wanted.

They caught Iago and dragged him back. Othello reeled at the sight of him. He stumbled towards his ensign and with a sudden cry of pitiful rage, he plunged his sword through him.

Iago regarded him in silence. Though his scheme was all exposed and he was finished, yet how perfect was the downfall of the Moor! Gone was all nobility, all honour, greatness, wisdom; here merely a creature who had killed an innocent upon a villain's word.

'I bleed, sir,' he taunted, 'but not killed.'

'Will you demand that demi-devil why he has ensnared my soul and body?' Othello whispered.

'Demand from me nothing. What you know, you know. From this time forth I will never speak another word,' Iago sneered.

Lodovico addressed the Moor. 'You must foresake this room and go with us. Your power and your command are taken over and Cassio rules in Cyprus. You shall remain a prisoner till the nature of your fault is known to the Venetian state.'

Othello stood once more quite still and calm. He moved towards the bed where Desdemona lay. For a long, silent moment, he gazed at her.

'Soft you: a word or two before you go,' he murmured to the assembled Venetians. 'I have done the state some service, and they know it. I pray you, in your letters, when you relate these unlucky deeds, speak of me as I am ... then must you speak of one that loved not wisely, but too well; of one not easily jealous, but being wrought, perplexed in the extreme, of one whose hand threw a pearl away.' He paused and in his eyes there was a gleam of secret knowledge. 'And say besides, that in Aleppo once, where a malignant Turk beat a Venetian and betrayed the state, I took the dog by the throat—' Before their eyes could catch his action or their hands could fly to stop him, he slid a secret dagger from his robes, 'and struck him, thus!' he thrust the dagger into his breast.

He spoke only to Desdemona now, so soft it was a whisper on the wind, his lips caressing hers. 'I kissed you before I killed you; no way but this; killing myself, to die upon a kiss.'

So ended the tale of Othello, Moor of Venice. It was the tale of Iago, too, whose work had reached its zenith in this night of savagery, and from whose sealed lips never spilled the reason for his villainy.

THE
TEMPEST

I T WAS THE FRENZY OF A RAGING ANIMAL, the fury of wind and sea that seized the ship. Thunder like the crack of doom; the flare of lightning across the decks. Flames engulfed the mast, a blazing furnace belched forth sailors wrestling with their burning vessel and its shrieking cargo: a king, a prince, a duke and lords.

But what did a royal cargo matter to that fury of wind and sea? Could a king's command throw back those mountainous waves? Could a lord's great wealth buy life or death before that tempest? There were no great or small, no rich or poor – only men, who shrieked before the thunder's power and knew their end had come.

The ship burned like a funeral pyre, split, was engulfed in a final, savage swell, and sank.

The watchers, high on a rocky headland, gazed in silence. Nothing but scattered splinters on a foaming sea. The one, a girl, stood pale, her huddled body speaking misery at each pitiful cry of helpless men.

Her companion stood, unmoving. There was no trace of pity, joy or sorrow on his face. It was an old face, etched with the lines of time and scored with a lifetime's wisdom. In his eyes there were glimmerings, flickerings, mysterious lights that echoed the silver of his hair and beard: gold, like the gold of a sunrise yet to come, red, like the fire that had consumed the ship, blue, like the sea seared by the lightning's flash ...

In his eyes there was a story yet untold. It stirred angrily within him as he watched the dying ship.

He wore a robe, dark, rich and heavy. The garment swayed, a strange, rhythmic movement of deep folds like secret caverns ripe with mysteries: fear, hope, knowledge, all were woven deep within its fabric, for there was magic in the web of it.

In his hand the old man held a staff, a gnarled wooden stick. Yet it was more, much more. It waited in his hand, as though it rested, as though no more than thought, no more than an eyelid's wink would fire its length with secret power. At his side there lay a book, red-bound and heavy, its pages worn with use, thumbed, scored, and learned, for they were pages saturated with the secrets of the enchanter's art.

The enchanter sighed, and turned towards the girl, whose pleading voice had broken through the dream that held him silent, watching.

'If by your art, my dearest father, you have put the wild waters in this roar, calm them,' his daughter begged. 'Poor souls, they perished ...'

Her father placed a calming hand against her cheek. 'Tell your piteous heart there's no harm done.' He looked towards the bay. The ship was gone. The winds were quieting. It had begun.

He drew his cloak about him, close, and held the staff before his face. He closed his eyes. And from the earth, the sky, the winds, he felt the powers flowing anew.

It had begun.

He turned towards his daughter. 'It is time.' He said it quietly, but with such force that instantly the girl grew quiet. 'I should inform you further,' he went on. 'Lend me your hand, and pluck my magic garments from me.'

Obediently the young girl grasped the robe and eased it from her father's shoulders. She laid it to one side.

'Lie there, my art,' her father murmured. He took her by the shoulders, led her to a rock, and bid her sit on it. 'Wipe your eyes: have comfort.'

Wonderingly she did so. Trustingly she waited. And so the enchanter began the tale that wrote its bitterness behind his eyes. This wreck that she had seen was conjured by his magic art. The storm was no more than a magician's fancy, drawn from sky and sea by Prospero, the enchanter. She stared in dread: was her beloved father a man who killed for fancy?

But no, his voice calmed her: no man was lost from that burned ship; every one still lived, as healthy as before the storm had caught them. Every man believed he had miraculously survived while all the others drowned. Yet, truly, not a single hair of any head was even wet. Prospero nodded with pride. Now was the beginning ...

It was also the end. Twelve years of preparation, in which every bone and sinew, every thought, hope, desire was sharpened to this moment. Twelve years now drawing to a close. The hour had come when he must tell Miranda why. It had begun a long time ago, in events long past, before ever they had come to dwell here on this island. Did she remember?

She had stirrings of faint memory, things far off but dream-like, the scattered remnants of a picture in a baby's mind: images of many women once attending her.

Prospero nodded. 'Twelve years ago, Miranda, your father was the Duke of Milan and a prince of power.'

Miranda frowned. 'Sir, are you not my father?'

Prospero gazed with eyes of love upon his innocent daughter. What would she make of the tale he had to tell; could her loving spirit understand such evil? His

face grew dark with memories: trust betrayed, love turned sour; greed, ambition, murder ...

Twelve years ago, he, Prospero, was Duke of Milan, ruler of the most powerful of all the states. Gentle Miranda, his daughter, was no more than a child of three, a princess. Duke Prospero of Milan had a brother, Antonio. In all the world Prospero loved no one as he loved Miranda and Antonio. He had trusted Antonio, as one could trust a beloved brother.

Prospero was a man of learning. More and more each day he grew fascinated by his studies, drawn deep into his books. Each day his library absorbed him more than the affairs of state and he left Antonio to rule the land for him. Antonio learned to revel in the control of men. There came a time when he no longer wanted just to act as duke, holding the keys of power in trust for Prospero. He yearned to be the duke, to wield that power, absolute power, for himself instead.

So the trusted brother Antonio, rotten with ambition, plotted with the King of Naples, a man long jealous of Milan's great wealth and power. One treacherous midnight, Antonio threw wide the city gates and let the enemy in. For this betrayal, the conquering King of Naples made Antonio Duke of Milan in Prospero's place.

Yet Antonio did not dare to kill his brother openly. By night he smuggled Prospero to the coast. With tiny Miranda, he cast him to the sea aboard a rotten carcass of a boat to let the pitiless waters do what Antonio dare not.

But they survived, through Prospero's strength and unexpected kindness from one man among the enemy, Gonzalo, who took pity on their plight and gave them food and water. Knowing how Prospero loved his books, he smuggled some of the most prized volumes to the boat.

'Here in this island we arrived ...' Prospero rose, and lifted the magic robe about his shoulders. He had returned to his beginning: the storm, the wreck.

Miranda waited. What reason could her father have for these?

Prospero smiled, and though to Miranda it was her father's gentle smile, yet there was nothing gentle in it. It told again of twelve long years of preparation for this moment; twelve long years to perfect his enchanter's arts. Now fortune smiled on him and brought his enemies to the shore of Prospero's island. The king on board that tormented ship was Alonso, King of Naples – who had overthrown a rightful duke and placed his vicious brother on the throne. The prince was none other than the King of Naples' son. There was the king's brother, too, Sebastian. Above all, there was Antonio, the man who stole a brother's dukedom and threw him and his child into the waves to die.

Prospero raised a hand to stop Miranda's cry. 'Here cease more questions.' He placed his hand upon her head, 'You are inclined to sleep.' Beneath the magician's spell, Miranda's eyes grew heavy, and obediently she slept.

Now Prospero stood alone. One hand held his robe outstretched, the other held the staff high in the wind. He lifted his face towards the sky, and closed his eyes.

'Come away, servant, come. I am ready now. Approach, my Ariel, come,' he sent the call out from his mind.

There was a shimmer through the air and swiftly his servant came, a thing of glancing light, of movements quick as sight, of sounds like murmuring brooks.

'All hail, great master! Hail! I come to answer thy best pleasure: be it to fly, to swim, to dive into the fire, to ride on the curled clouds ...'

Eagerly the master greeted him. Had the tempest been performed exactly as he asked; was every instruction followed?

Eagerly the servant-spirit answered: flying as flames, he had blazed along the boat, brought lightning, thunderclaps, the mountainous waves, till all on board were mad with terror and all except the sailors plunged into the sea to escape the fires. First had been the king's son, Ferdinand, crying, 'Hell is empty, and all the devils are here!'

And yet – the master-stroke – they were all safe, all dry on land, not a single hair was damaged, garments glossier than before. They were scattered in groups across the island, each certain that all others must be dead.

All had been done by Ariel exactly as Prospero demanded.

The king's son, Ferdinand, was brought ashore alone. He was now lodged in a deserted corner of the island, plunged in deep melancholy, mourning the loss of father, friends and ship alike. The sailors were all safely stowed aboard the ship. It nestled (with no trace of fire) in a sheltered corner of the bay, hidden by curtaining mists. Below her decks the sailors slept a deep, charmed sleep.

Prospero sighed. All faithfully done. 'But there's more work,' he spoke urgently.

Yet Ariel was restless. Prospero had promised freedom when this day's work was done. Twelve years Ariel had served the enchanter faithfully against that promise.

But now the reminder angered Prospero. 'Do you forget from what a torment I did free you?' he thundered. 'Have you forgotten the foul witch Sycorax?'

And Ariel trembled. Sycorax, once ruler of this island, had shut him painfully in a pine tree for refusing to obey her foul commands. There he had writhed for twelve agonising years.

'It was my art that made the pine gape wide and let you out!' Prospero's call to loyalty hung, threatening, in the air. And now the air grew still, for Ariel was silent.

Then, 'I thank thee, master,' came the whisper on the breeze. 'I will obey commands, and do my spiriting gently.'

'Do so,' the sorcerer's voice grew gentle too. 'And after two days I will discharge you. Go now. Transform yourself into a nymph of the sea.'

The spirit flew, and Prospero woke Miranda. There was still more to do, more he had planned. 'We'll visit Caliban my slave,' he told her, and hurried her towards a hovel crouching, dark and evil-smelling, below a jutting rock.

'What, ho! Slave! Caliban! You earth, you! Speak!' his voice rang out. 'Come forth, I say!' Prospero grew angry.

A misshapen figure stumbled into view. The mouth drew back on snarling teeth, reddened eyes burned at his tormenter, for Caliban hated Prospero with a ravenous passion. Yet he feared him more, for any disobedience to the enchanter's will was swiftly punished with jabbing pains to torture every bone and sinew of his twisted body.

'This island's mine, by Sycorax my mother,' he hissed. 'When you came first, you stroked me and made much of me and then I showed you all the qualities of the isle, the fresh springs, the barren place and fertile.' He fixed a haunted eye on Prospero. 'Cursed be I that did so! All the charms of Sycorax, toads, beetles, bats,

light on you! You taught me language, and my profit on it is, I know how to curse you!' And the creature that had once been lord of all the island, waited, sullen, to take his orders from the enchanter.

For Prospero had need of Caliban, just as he needed the spirit Ariel ...

◊ ◊ ◊

There was the lilt of music, the whirr of Ariel upon the breeze, a song that floated in the air and caught the listener and drew him on.

'Come unto these yellow sands ...' the spirit sang.

The listener followed, stumbling to keep pace, losing and finding the sounds again, drawn on, ever on towards the enchanter's cave.

It was Prince Ferdinand, the King of Naples's son, a fine gentleman, tall, young and strong, richly-dressed and handsome, though his eager face was shadowed with his sorrows. He had been sitting on a bank mourning his father's death when strange music had crept by upon the waters and snaked into his mind.

'Sure it waits upon some god of the island,' the young man breathed. There – the sounds again, floating about his head, now to this side, now the other ...

'Full fathom five thy father lies;
Of his bones are coral made;
Those are pearls that were his eyes ...' sang Ariel.

In awe the young man stopped. This could be no earthly sound, no sound from human voice!

Miranda, seated as her father placed her, saw the young man enter the clearing before their cave and leapt to her feet. In her young life she had seen only her father's long white beard and wrinkled face and the twisted form of Caliban. 'What is it?' she gasped to Prospero. 'A spirit? It is a spirit!'

'No,' Prospero smiled at her. 'It eats and sleeps and has such senses as we have. This gallant was in the wreck. He has lost his fellows and strays about to find them.'

Miranda feasted her eyes on the figure. She drank in the sight. Surely a god!

She was captured, and Prospero was pleased. All was as he desired, all as he planned. Secret thanks he sent to invisible Ariel hovering near, 'Spirit, fine spirit! I'll free you within two days for this!'

Ferdinand was a much-travelled young prince, used to the rich beauties who graced the royal courts of Europe. Yet this vision of a windblown girl caught in a sunlit glade, fixed him in wonderment to the spot. Never had he seen such beauty!

It glowed like the sun itself. Surely this must be the goddess of the isle, she who conjured enchanted music from the air!

But then the goddess spoke, told him she was nothing but a girl, and miraculously, he understood the words! In relief Prince Ferdinand tumbled out the story of the wreck and all hands lost with it, his father's death, who he was, who else was on the ship, of Antonio, Duke of Milan ...

At his usurping brother's name, pangs of anger filled Prospero like the hot pains he cast on Caliban. But there was much else to be done, before the end. First (his prime design) his powers must be used on Ferdinand, all for Miranda. Love already flowed between these two: every look between them spoke of it. For this he had drawn Ferdinand to the isle. But love could be misplaced, and love could be betrayed, and Prospero's life was testimony to this. Before Ferdinand could win Miranda as a wife, his love must stand the test of strength and constancy and truth and honesty. Love must be fought for.

And so he set the prince a task to prove his worth – and a trial to test his daughter's constancy. 'Come!' he ordered Ferdinand. 'I'll chain your neck and feet together: seawater you shall drink; your food shall be the fresh-brook muscles, withered roots and husks in which the acorn cradled. Follow!' and he gave his face a look more terrible than he had shown before.

It did not frighten Ferdinand. The more Miranda pleaded for Ferdinand with all her heart, the more Prospero frowned with stern, unbending harshness. Yet the young prince bore his trials bravely, declared that he could bear all lightly if he could see the sweet face of Miranda just once a day!

'It works,' breathed Prospero. And then to Ariel, he promised through his mind, 'You shall be as free as mountain winds: but then exactly do all points of my command.'

'To the syllable,' came Ariel's wind-blown music ...

◇ ◇ ◇

In a sunlit glade they gathered, a king, nobles, lords, all saved from watery death, all gorgeously attired in silks, brocades and velvets unstained by salt-sea wave. One old man, a wizened counsellor to the King of Naples, was hopeful. They were not dead: a miracle!

But Alonso, King of Naples, was plunged in misery. His son was dead – he had a vision of him wound grotesquely with seaweed on the ocean bed ...

'Weigh our sorrow with our comfort,' the old counsellor, Gonzalo, urged. In fact, he was that same Gonzalo who saved Prospero and Miranda from certain death twelve years before.

'Peace!' Alonso begged him.

'He receives comfort like cold porridge,' observed Alonso's brother, Sebastian, nastily. For Sebastian there were no comforts here, between wilting kings and counsellors who chattered like ancient parrots. But old Gonzalo gazed at the green, lush, sunlit place, drew the soft winds deep into his lungs, and thought dreamily of the world that might be built in such a paradise: no riches, no poverty, all men equal, all women too, all innocent and pure; no sovereignty ...

'Yet he would be king of it,' sneered Sebastian, who thought a world without riches to be seized would be a poor, boring world indeed.

Prospero had heard enough: he sent Ariel among them to float unseen and fill the glade with mournful music, dark tones to fill their eyes with heaviness, drag down their limbs, till one by one they slept.

Not all of them. There was another scene in Prospero's drama shortly to be acted: Sebastian and Antonio remained awake.

To a discerning eye, these two could not be easily told apart. Antonio was a brother turned a thief, betrayer of a brother's trust. Sebastian was brother to a king, shortly to betray a brother's trust, for he was a cold, ambitious man. Here they were, marooned on a deserted island beyond reach of any court or palace, far from the powers of Naples or Milan. Here, where they had secured neither food nor drink nor shelter, nor any means of getting off the island (ignorant of the ship still hidden in the mists) where life might rest upon one man's help to another, these two remained true to their own natures: they saw only one means of advancement, even in the sunshine of an island basking in the sea. First Antonio and then Sebastian, quickly convinced by his faster-thinking fellow, cast their eyes on their companions, fast asleep, and on a weak-kneed king and dream-filled counsellor. Swiftly they concluded that if both were killed (Prince Ferdinand being already dead) why then Sebastian could be King of Naples, and Antonio rise to power with him. Two swift murders – and the power would be theirs.

From afar the enchanter heard. Again the games of power played with life and death as toys! But this time Gonzalo, once his friend would be the loser. In no more than the blinking of an eye, Ariel was sent to wake Gonzalo and the king.

Caught with drawn swords and guilty faces, Sebastian and Antonio muttered of bellowing bulls (or was it roaring lions) against which they drew their weapons.

A glitter fired the enchanter's eyes. All as he remembered, all as he designed.

◇ ◇ ◇

Caliban toiled along the beach beneath the load of wood, cursing, spitting, moaning with every grunting movement. Hatred for his master drove him like a furnace. His brain ached with memories of years of torment under Prospero. Spirits conjured – now like biting apes, now like hissing snakes – a thousand agonies from pricks and pinches, pains and cramps.

He stopped. A figure came towards him: jingling cap and tattered, flapping colours. It chattered, stumbled, mumbled, cowered, trembled, shook a bony fist towards the sky. To Caliban, all figures were but spirits sent by Prospero to torture him. In terror he fell to the ground and flung his tattered cloak across his head, in vain hope he would be invisible.

The figure was another bewildered survivor from the shipwreck that never happened: Trinculo, ageing jester to the King of Naples, miraculously alive, but facing, he believed, imminent destruction from freshly brewing storms.

More thunder, distant, rumbling closer, ominous. Trinculo winced and clutched his arms about his skinny shoulders, running.

He saw the bundle on the ground and lurched to a halt. He pushed it cautiously with one toe. Dead or alive? A fish: it smelt like a fish, a very ancient fish-like smell ...

A roll of thunder made the ageing jester jump. Weighing the stench of a fish-like dead-or-alive creature against the terrors of lightning that burned a ship to cinders, he chose the fish, and with his bony nose pinched tight against the stench, he crept under the hairy cloak.

Caliban felt the nearness of a torturing spirit sent by Prospero and lay rigid, playing dead.

Towards this four-legged, four-armed hairy bundle on the beach, there came another apparition, one that swayed and tripped, hiccupped, swigged from a bottle, and lurched on. Stephano, the King of Naples' butler, floated to land on a wine barrel, had been filling his bloated stomach ever since. Now he stumbled across the hairy, smelly bundle. He gave it a hefty kick, reeled with the effort, burped and flopped with a gurgling squelch into the sand.

Whereupon Caliban howled, dreading some new and horrible torture from the spirits.

The drunken butler pushed his bleared eyes close to the stinking bundle. A four-armed, four-legged howling creature! Some island monster in a fever? Stephano lurched to a sitting position. An island monster, cured and tamed, might yet be taken back to Naples. What a present for an emperor! Stephano raised his bottle to the threatening clouds and drank to the idea, then prodded the monster.

Caliban groaned. 'Do not torment me. I'll bring my wood home faster,' he begged beneath the cloak.

'He's in a fit now,' announced Stephano. 'He shall taste of my bottle.' He nodded sagely, for the bottle was cure for any ill. He stuck it in the monster's mouth, and leapt in shock to find it was a monster of such skill that it could suddenly, upon drinking, produce two voices, one in the top end (where a man might expect to hear a voice) and one in the bottom end that, when filled up with wine, miracle of miracles, called him by his own name!

Being a brave man, he pulled at the monster's smaller legs and discovered his

good friend Trinculo. At which the two friends danced for joy, comparing notes on escape from watery graves.

Caliban was feeling a warm inner glow that seemed uncannily connected to that bottle. Wonderingly he gazed at it and the portly man in tattered breeches who nursed the magic potion.

'Have you not dropped from heaven?' he asked.

'Out of the moon, I do assure you,' chortled Stephano.

It was enough for Caliban: this was a god with potions that could lift a man from earth and make him fly. He fell to his knees before his god, 'I'll show you every fertile inch of the island: I will kiss your foot,' he pledged, and did so. 'I'll show you the best springs, I'll pluck you berries, I'll fish for you ...' And in his overflowing love he offered the god all the riches of this kingdom, as once he had to Prospero.

'A most ridiculous monster, to make a wonder of a poor drunkard,' observed Trinculo the jester, blinking.

'Lead the way,' cried Stephano. 'Trinculo, the king and all our company being drowned, we will inherit here. This will be our kingdom! Bear my bottle,' he said to Caliban, majestically, and Caliban took the bottle as though it were a delicate jewel nestling on a gilded cushion, and held it up aloft, and led them, singing ...

'Ban, Ban Cacaliban,
Has a new master: get a new man ...
Freedom, hey-day! Hey-day, freedom!'

◇ ◇ ◇

To test Miranda in her love for Ferdinand, Prospero had set him Caliban's work. Did handsome youths in gorgeous clothes, transformed to filth and sweat and rags, still shine for her? Or did Ferdinand at dirty work become a Caliban in her young eyes? Ferdinand toiled at fetching and carrying logs, thousand upon thousand. Being a king's son and unfitted for work of any kind, he struggled beneath the burden. Miranda wept to see him so: she offered to do it for him; she shared his misery. But he was valiant: driven on by Miranda's wistful adoration, he manfully endured his trials.

Prospero was satisfied. Their love was not destroyed by harshness; it grew bolder. Ferdinand swore he prized and honoured Miranda above all else, and Miranda answered with love. Prospero almost wept with joy. Before this day was over, Miranda would be Ferdinand's wife – the future Queen of Naples. Soon this act of Prospero's drama could be closed.

◇ ◇ ◇

Stephano was playing king, and passed the bottle. Caliban drank, adored his god, and passed the bottle. Trinculo drank, jeered at Caliban, and passed the bottle. Caliban told them of his master who had by sorcery seized the island.

'From me he got it,' Caliban cried, and stared through desperate eyes at god Stephano. 'If you will revenge it on him, you shall be lord of it and I'll serve you!'

Planted in Stephano's brain, the idea was good. Decorated here and there with something of the customs of this master, and something of his possessions, and something of his pretty daughter, the idea was even better. 'Monster, I will kill this man: his daughter and I will be king and queen, and Trinculo and yourself shall be viceroys.'

They shook hands on it, and passed the bottle, and Stephano sang the song again that he had been teaching Caliban.

'Flout 'em and scout 'em,
And scout 'em, and flout 'em;
Thought is free.'

To their consternation the tune was changing! Lilting pipes drowned out their merry verse, and though they struggled to hold a course, the ghostly music overwhelmed and terrified them.

'Are you afraid?' asked Caliban curiously. 'Be not afraid. The isle is full of noises, sounds and sweet airs, that give delight and hurt not.' A dreaming peace had come upon the creature as he spoke; as though he melted once again into this island that was his.

'This will prove a brave kingdom to me, where I shall have my music for nothing,' Stephano yelled, and gathered more courage from the bottle.

'When Prospero is destroyed,' Caliban reminded him.

'The sound is going away,' cried Trinculo, bolder for the reminder of their paradise to come. 'Let's follow it and after do our work!'

'Lead, monster,' Stephano waved Caliban on, 'we'll follow ...'

But Ariel, musician of the air, had heard their plot, and swift as a salt-sea breeze across the bay had carried news to Prospero: Caliban the slave had found a god with a faded, jingling henchman by his side, and these three lurched towards him, bent on murder for the kingdom of the island.

Again the game of power was played, with life and death as toys.

◇ ◇ ◇

With aching limbs and heavy heart, the King of Naples sank to rest. Even the sea mocked their search for the king's son, Ferdinand. All the lords and nobles faltered, too – even Gonzalo was beyond cheerful words; his old bones ached too much with tramping. Sebastian and Antonio, though, hovered close, preparing for their plot. As soon as opportunity was there (Sebastian nodded to Antonio). Tonight, Antonio urged Sebastian.

Their secret dialogue broke off: strange, solemn sounds, like deep murmurs, were rising from the earth. They moved nervously together. The air grew misty. They huddled closer. From the gleaming centre of the mists came twisting shapes – half animal, half human, grotesque and ugly. Yet they smiled, bore a banquet to the centre of the glade, table upon table piled with food, and then with nods and bows they melted back into air and only the echo of the music floated on.

But they had left the feast. King and lords stared round nervously. King and lords awaited further happenings. The glade was quiet. The lords were hungry – hungrier by the minute. Sebastian was all for eating. Alonso drew back anxiously.

They moved towards the laden tables cautiously.

There was a clap of thunder and lightning seared across the glade. A great bird swooped between them, a monstrous giant with hag-like human face and the body of a taloned vulture. The vast wings smote the table and instantly the banquet vanished.

'You are three men of sin,' the apparition cried. The thundering voice was agony in their ears. 'On this island where man doth not inhabit, you amongst men being most unfit to live, I have made you mad!'

Sebastian and Antonio drew swords.

'You fools!' the terrible voice rang out. 'I and my fellows are ministers of Fate: your swords may as well wound the loud winds, or kill the waters, as diminish one feather in my plume!'

The voice rose to the rumbling of an earthquake, trees and rocks shook with its wrath. 'But remember—' The warning shivered in the air. 'Remember! You three did supplant good Prospero from Milan: for which foul deed, the powers have incensed the seas and shores, yes, all the creatures, against your peace. They have bereft thee, Alonso of thy son, and by me they do pronounce a lingering torture, worse than any death, shall step by step attend you and your ways.'

There was a roll of thunder, so deafening and the light so blinding, that they hid their heads. And when they looked again, the bird had gone.

In his wake soft music played to mock them, the shimmering spirits of the air returned, and before their helpless eyes and hands, taunting, the spirits danced and carried out the table.

The glade was empty now, filled only with their terror.

Invisible above, Prospero, waited. Now let the terror work. Now let their agony of fear bore madness deep within each villainous heart ...

◇ ◇ ◇

The time had come for Prospero to free Ferdinand. Being so close now to the end, the enchanter wished to give one final gift to these young people, to reveal the wonders of his powers, before the end, to them.

He closed his eyes, and through his mind he sent the call: 'Spirits, which by my art I now call up,' he cried, and rejoiced as his many spirits thronged about the united couple. They danced in celebration of the lovers: spirits of all the island's secret places, of the woods and trees, the streams and lapping seas, of hill and valley, sky and earth ...

Then he froze. A thought, ice cold, had shot into his brain. In the warmth of the young people's love he had forgotten Caliban and the conspiracy against his life. With that memory, warm visions of love and plenty he had conjured up were gone. Ferdinand and Miranda stared in dismay at Prospero, grown dark with bitterness again.

Prospero moved swiftly to comfort them.

'Be cheerful. Our revels now are ended. These, our actors, were all spirits and are melted into air! We are such stuff as dreams are made of, and our little life is rounded with a sleep ...'

But Caliban was coming. Summoning Ariel, Prospero gave commands. Light as the sea-blown breeze, the spirit-servant flew and returned. In his arms rich garments gleamed with all the colours of the rainbow. Prospero had charmed a storm, a wreck, a spirit-feast, to confuse and madden a treacherous king and villainous lords;

he had brought forth a spirits' dance of blessing for young lovers. Now, to thwart the drunken murderers, he chose the vanity of gaudy clothes to deck a would-be king ...

◇　◇　◇

They were not so jovial as before, Stephano, Caliban and Trinculo. Ghostly music had led them on a stumbling dance through thorns and briars, and now their bottle lay beneath the rancid scum of some filthy gurgling pond. Trinculo whined, Stephano bellowed, and Caliban was terrified that Prospero would hear them.

But Trinculo saw the clothes. With a cry of ecstasy he fell upon them. Garments for a king, finery for a king's minister, riches beyond a jester's dreams!

'Let it alone, you fool,' hissed Caliban. 'It is trash.'

But already a battle royal raged between a would-be king and would-be minister: cavorting, squabbling, flourishing, snatching, heads, arms, legs, thrusting in and out of sleeves and tearing necklines.

'I will have none of it,' yelled Caliban, 'we shall lose our time, and all be turned to barnacles or apes!'

But it was neither apes nor barnacles for them. Blood-curdling yowls, the snapping jaws of ravenously baying hunting dogs erupted from the forest, and before the snarling terror of those phantom beasts, the would-be killers fled.

Prospero and Ariel watched their quarry run. 'At this hour lie at my mercy all mine enemies,' triumphant Prospero spoke. 'Shortly shall all my labours end. And you, Ariel, shall have the air at freedom: for a little, follow, and do me service ...'

The spirit bowed his head; the final act was drawing near – and after, liberty.

◊ ◊ ◊

'Now does my project gather to a head: my charms crack not – my spirits obey.' Prospero stood ready. Round his shoulders swayed his magic robe. By his side stood Ariel. 'How's the day?' Prospero murmured to his faithful spirit servant.

'On the sixth hour; at which time, you said our work should cease.'

'I did say so, when first I raised the tempest.'

Since then: a king and treacherous brothers had been maddened with their guilt and fear, imprisoned at his will, locked fast by charms.

The final power. His they were, for life or death. The final choice now lay before him.

'Your charm so strongly works on them, that if you now beheld them, your affections would become tender,' Ariel's music reached into his mind. He stood quietly. 'Do you think so, spirit?' he asked.

'Mine would, sir, were I human,' the spirit answered.

Silence grew about the enchanter and his tender servant-spirit. The final choice must now be made. But Prospero was listening to Ariel's music.

Finally he spoke. 'Go release them, Ariel,' the enchanter said. 'My charms I'll break, their senses I'll restore, and they shall be themselves.'

Joyfully, Ariel sped away. Prospero stood alone. He closed his eyes, and spread his arms out wide so that the robe swirled, rich with magic powers. 'I have bedimmed the noontide sun, called forth the mutinous winds, and between the green sea and the blue vault of the sky I have set roaring war: to the dread rattling thunder have I given fire ... and by the roots plucked up the pine and cedar ... graves, at my command have waked their sleepers, opened and let them forth ...'

But here would be the end. He knew that now. Here, when the final act was over.

He drew a magic circle, and into it they came, the maddened king, the staring brothers, the bewildered lords, held in Prospero's enchantment, silent, asleep, awaiting the final vengeance.

Now they must see him as he was, when all began: as Prospero, one-time Duke of Milan. Swiftly, singing, for his liberty was nearing and he danced with joy, Ariel helped the old man to remove the robes of Prospero the enchanter. Now he stood as Prospero, the Duke.

Slowly, with no violence, Prospero released his victims from their sleep.

They stared in disbelief: Prospero, long believed dead, come back from the grave! Their minds, a few moments ago twisting in crazed terror, calm and clear again! There followed a scene of such bewilderment and awe, recognitions, explanations, grief, remorse, apologies and reconciliation, as the island had never seen before, nor would it ever again. Alonso, King of Naples, who had long felt an inward torture for the deeds committed twelve long years ago, wept for sorrow at his villainy and begged forgiveness. Gonzalo was in ecstasies of joy, relief and amazement all in one.

Antonio and Sebastian, who in a trice had understood that Prospero knew all and could, with but a single word, betray their villainy to Alonso, now faced the ultimate of judges: their own consciences, newly-sharpened by the terrors of this island magic.

From them all, Prospero had one demand: the restoration of his dukedom, lands, wealth and rights.

Alonso, of course, still mourned the loss of Ferdinand: Prospero drew back the curtains of his cave and revealed Miranda. Quietly, and needing nothing more, she played at chess with none other than Prince Ferdinand. More wonderment, embracing, joy, and explanations.

Miranda stared in rapture at the glorious array of gilded lords. 'How beauteous mankind is!' she cried. 'Oh brave new world, that has such people in it!'

'It is new to you,' said Prospero, with a lifetime's weary knowledge.

They still mourned the loss of sailors, captain, ship. One by one they were produced, lifted through the balmy air and placed before them by invisible Ariel.

'Was it well done?' whispered Ariel to Prospero.

'Bravely,' whispered Prospero to Ariel. 'You shall be free. Set Caliban and his companions free; untie the spell.'

And so to the final revelation: the hapless trio stumbled in, limply hung with stolen clothes, cowed and sheepish now. Caliban, expecting vicious punishment, found in Prospero a new master, decked in unknown finery, and generous in forgiveness. Instantly he transferred his adoration to this better master, and wondered how he had ever adored a drunkard as a god.

So now, instead of vengeance, hospitality was all that Prospero offered. On the morrow they would embark for Naples to see the marriage of Ferdinand and Miranda – the final bond of reconciliation tied. Then Prospero would turn for home – for Milan.

'I promise you calm seas, auspicious gales,' the enchanter murmured. And in his mind he called for the last time to Ariel. 'My Ariel, chick, that is your charge: then to the elements be free ...'

There was a flutter in the breeze as of a dragonfly's wings, and with a whisper of farewell and love to Prospero, the spirit flew to liberty.

◇　◇　◇

Prospero stood alone, high on the rocky headland. Ariel and Caliban were free: one to the winds, and one to his island paradise.

Prospero had planned his magic all for vengeance: yet in the final hour it had brought him face to face with tenderness and charity. In the magic circle drawn for punishment, he had seen his victims' misery was no less terrible than his own twelve years before, his ruthless use of power no better than the abuse he had suffered at their hands. That was the final music Ariel had played for him.

So now the sea would take his magic and bury it deep. First his robe, and then his book, and finally his staff, broken in two, he cast into the waves. For that brief moment, as he saw them flying from his hands, there was unutterable despair. He was a man again, no more than a man. Gone was the magic that had given him power over earth, air, fire, water, life and death, and over an infinity of dreams.

But after the despair came a new peace: as a man he had the power of choice, of knowledge, understanding, compassion, pity, love. And in that there was untold richness, glory, hope – and dreams.

◇ ◇ ◇